Spring Break with an Ohio Boss

By National Best-Selling Author

Chaniqué J

Synopsis

Casanae and Neoshi, lifelong best friends, are living their best lives preparing for, yet again, another hot girl summer. Things take a slight curve when they cross paths with Marco and Dave, from the same city but completely different paths of life.

Girls just wanna have fun. Whether it's for spring break or because it's only natural to enjoy the sunshine, quality time and excitement of a vacation, especially in the company of your best friend.

Will the flings and sparks that were created during spring break be enough to keep these two couples together. Or will the secrets, confrontation, and law be enough to tear apart the bonds they created. Everything isn't always peaches and cream when dealing with a Boss, especially not from OHIO!

Word to my readers……

I just wanna give thanks! Not only to the man above all! To my Family, Friends and Supports. I appreciate every one of you. I can only hope that my absence has made the heart grow fonder, instead of forgotten.

It's safe to say my passion for writing has changed over the years. I still enjoy creating stories and sharing them with my readers; it just takes so much more out of me mentally, compared to when I first started. If I could, I would continue to write a book a month like I once did but I can't. I hope you all enjoy this book just as you have the others I've written thus far. Thank you for your continued support and dedication.

Sincerely Chanique J

Spring Break with an Ohio Boss

Casanae

"Why you holding up the damn bar? If you don't bring your ass out to this dance floor, I know something." Neoshi complained as she scattered her ass back to the dance floor.

Something told me not to wear no damn heels out tonight in the first place. Listening to Neo's eager ass talking about we had to be on some grown and sexy shit. Now I'm regretting it. I understood it was a grand opening at AJ's Place, but the crowd seemed just the same as all the other clubs in our area. The crowd seems to be a mixture between classy and ratty. My Air Max 95's would've been sufficient enough. A pair of joggers and a nice form fitting tee shirt would suit me a lot better than the damn polyester skintight dress with six-inch heels I had on.

Chasing my double shot of 1738 with cranberry gave me just enough strength to take my tail to the dance floor to accompany Neo. Doing my little two steps was home for the night, I worked a nice twelve-hour shift on my feet and right now even my two steps was doing too much. The 1738 was kicking in, and feeling the sweat beads beginning to form on my forehead and upper lip was my cue to have a seat for a second. I had no intentions on getting sweaty tonight, just sitting pretty. The combination of 1738 and music wasn't going to allow Neo to sit still, and if I kept up with her liquor intake tonight it wouldn't be for me either.

As I took my seat at the bar near where we were originally posted, I noticed the bartender heading in my direction with drinks in hand. Since I tipped her good for our first round, I assumed she was coming back to service me. When she placed four drinks in front of me, I eyed her in confusion.

"These were sent over here for you and your girl from the gentleman in VIP by the DJ booth." The bartender stated with a smile before walking away. As bad as I wanted to immediately turn around and scan the VIP section for the nigga trying to get some ass, I played it smooth and called over another bartender to bring me a whole bottle. Although I said I wasn't drinking much tonight I had to show the mystery man in VIP I wasn't a cheap shot type of chick. He had to come harder than that if he wanted my attention.

"Why you order shots and a bottle?" Neo questioned.

"I didn't. I ordered the bottle when some nigga in VIP sent over two double shots for us."

"What nigga in VIP sent over two double shots?" Neo started looking around the club focusing in on each VIP section.

"I don't know which one sent the shit. I just know that the bartender said he was in the section by the DJ booth."

"I mean, it's like twenty niggas up there. How the hell we supposed to know who sent it. Well whoever the nigga is thank you, but you got to come harder than that." Neo said before putting her shot in the air towards the VIP section and taking it to the head. As she took her free shot to the head, I turned facing the same direction and refilled my cup with our bottle.

As the music blasted through the speakers, track after track, we continued to drink shots back to back until we were beyond buzzed. As we finished off the bottle, I knew I was drunk but that's right where Neo wanted to be; the night was only beginning for her now. When I flagged the bartender down to request a bottle of water, she returned with not only my two bottles of water but more liquor.

Buying that bottle to prove a point was the wrong move on my behalf because whoever the VIP nigga was sent over not one but two bottles of 1738 for us. I guess us buying a bottle and facing VIP while drinking it rubbed him the wrong way. I wasn't trying to shoot any shots, but I needed any nigga sending drinks my way to know it's going take more than two punk ass shots to get my attention. There was no way in hell me and Neo would finish two more bottles of 1738. I mean I like to drink and I'm no lightweight, but I still need my kidney and liver to function tomorrow when all this is done and over with.

Our original plan was to step out, sit cute, and take our ass home before last call. Two bottles of liquor, four bottles of water and hours later, here we were as the DJ cut the music off to announce last call. The was our cue to head in the direction of the exit before the entire crowd did.

"What the hell we going do with a whole bottle?" Neo slurred.

"Not finish it!" I said and busted out into giggles. We were both for sure drunk, and there was no questioning that.

"Well where the hell the rest of the bottle going to go. I ain't bout to give it back. Da Fuck!" Neo said as she made an attempt to pour her another cup and spilled it on the counter of the bar.

"You ain't bout to drink it either obviously." I joked.

"Aye Excuse me!" Neo yelled out to get the bartender's attention.

"Can we get a Togo Bottle, please and thank you!" Neo slurred but was serious as fuck.

"What you mean a to go bottle?" The tender questioned with a puzzled look on her face.

"You know like a Togo cup, but instead a bottle. Ain't no fucking way we are going to be able to finish this bottle and I for damn sure ain't leaving it here and it's paid for.

"Aww no, I don't think we are allowed to do that." The bartender said with a slight giggle.

"Well, what the hell you expect me to do, just give my liquor away. Nah, that's definitely not an option." Neo giggled right back with her but was serious as hell.

"Girl it ain't like we paid for it, leave it here. We don't need the shit no way." I suggested, although I understood where Neo was coming from.

"I don't give a shit who paid for it, it's ours." Neo said and giggled her ass back to the dance floor.

"Take the whole damn bottle; we had enough!" I said as I poured our final cups with the bottle before pushing it away in the direction of the bartender for her to take it.

Pour up the whole damn seal, I'mma get lazy

I got the mojo deals, we been trapping like the 80's

She sucked a nigga soul, got the Cash App

Told em wipe a nigga nose, say slat, slat

Roddy Rich "The Box" played as my vision blurred while Neo and I twerked together on the dance floor.

Marco

Last night was a damn movie, for sure. I wasn't expecting my first night on the scene to be so damn lit. Being home from the Feds after a six-year bid felt damn good but this is a whole new lifestyle for me. It had been almost two months since I touched down and was considered a free man but last night was the first time I stepped foot into any type of public gathering since before I got locked up. When I left, we were kicking it to "Lifestyle" by Rich Gang. Let me try to cut that shit on now and pull up. Muthafuckas going be side-eyeing me like it's George Clinton's "Atomic Dog".

So much changed in the past six years; it's like, I'm in a whole new world. The streets ain't the same, niggas changed, even the bitches done switched up on me. I called myself doing a nice gesture by sending some drinks over to a chick who caught my attention but that wasn't good enough. The next moment I looked up and saw the bitch standing with a friend with an entire bottle in her hand like she was trying to insult the drinks I sent to her. Instead of coming down from the VIP section that was set up for my official welcome home little get up, I told the bottle girl to send them each a bottle of whatever they were drinking next time around instead of shots.

I wasn't going to play cat and mouse with no saditty ass bitch, but I wanted her and her home girl to know I could be just as arrogant. My money long and anyone who knows me knows that, so it wasn't shit to send a bottle to begin with. I just ain't know that's how bitches were doing it, now days.

"Nigga, I thought you ass was gon' be down for the count after last night." Dave said as he flopped down on the sectional across from where I was sitting.

"I probably should be laying down still, but my body won't allow me. After being on a set schedule for so long it's like I got an automatic alarm clock. I got up a little after seven and been up since. I did my little workout, hopped in the shower and been down here playing around on this damn phone."

"Nigga, fuck all that. I would've been playing around in somebody damn drive through if I got up that early. Fuck a workout; my damn stomach is in my back; I knew I should've grabbed some wings from the club last night for this morning. My drunk ass forgot all about it after too many drinks." He complained.

"Them bitches was looking good den a bitch. I should've ordered some, but I wasn't even focused on no damn food. I was in a whole 'nother zone."

"Shit, you and me both. All I saw was ass and titties flopping everywhere. The last thing a nigga was gon' remember was food. How I managed to still not slide in no pussy is beyond me at this point." Dave said as he brushed his hand down his face in frustration.

"You and me both. I eyed something nice, but the bitch was acting bad and bougie."

Dave chuckled at my comment. "What you mean by that?" he questioned while still laughing.

"I sent the bitch a few drinks and the bitch turned and faced the section drinking out a damn bottle like my shots wasn't good enough." I said with sarcasm in my voice.

"These hoes be showing out. I would've straight gone and got my drink back from the bitch. Fuck all that." I couldn't help but laugh at this foo.

"Nigga, fuck I look like walking over to the bitch and telling her refill my cup now since she brought a bottle?"

"I don't give two fucks how I would've looked. Bitch I need a refund since you too good." Dave replied.

"Not a muthafuckin refund. You wide as fuck for that one."

"Call it what you want, but the bitch would've never tried that shit again. Teach her ungrateful ass to just drink the shit and be coo next time." I couldn't do shit besides shake my head and laugh at him. As I got up from the sectional and headed into the kitchen for a bottle water, I noticed some noise coming from the basement area.

"You brought somebody home last night?" I questioned as I walked back into the living room.

"No, her ass brought me home." Dave said while shaking his head.

"What you mean? We rode home together, nigga!" I said while laughing.

"Man, that's Nyia's ass. I went over there on some last resort pussy type shit and she got me." Nyia is Dave's baby mom. Them two been on and off since high school. The nigga wont commit to her for shit but won't leave her alone either. Up until last night, they were on one of their off seasons last I checked.

"What you mean she got you?"

"Man, I don't know. Last thing I remember was her telling me she wasn't sucking shit if she couldn't even come stay with me at my crib. Somehow we ended up here, and I still ain't get no sloppy from her stupid ass."

"Wait, you mean to tell me she wasn't going, unless you brought her back here. What the hell was that supposed to prove?"

"I don't know. Shit, she been complaining ever since I moved about not knowing where I lived. Last night I was so damn thirsty to feel her tonsils I ain't give a fuck and now the bitch gon' feel some type of way thinking shit back sweet between us and it ain't. What she doesn't know is the moment I pick my whip up from her crib I'm putting her ass on the block list this time. She got me fucked up." Dave said as he stood from the couch while stretching.

"Aye Nyia, it's time to get your ass up! I got moves to make!" Dave yelled in the direction of the basement." I wondered why the hell he had her downstairs in the basement, and he had a fully furnished bedroom.

Instead of giving that nigga an audience and remaining in the living room, I decided to head upstairs and get dressed for the day. Saturdays are normally my casual days when I just kick back and do whatever the wind blows me to do, so there wasn't much on the agenda for me. After grabbing a pair of black Rock Revival jeans, a solid white V-neck polo, and my all-white Air Force One's I was ready to make some moves to get my day started.

Unlike most niggas my age, I didn't get out and run straight back to the streets. Instead, I used that time while locked up to boss up mentally. Wasn't no way, I planned to waste my time catching another case to be back behind bars. There's not an ounce of bitch in my blood, but I ain't trying to go back down that road ever again. Being careless and young minded is what landed me behind bars in the first place. Trying to be the man instead of a man taught me a hard lesson that cost me six years of my life. Anything in life can be replaced, but my youth I'll never get back. I lost and gained a lot while behind them bars.

The things and people I lost helped me to appreciate everything I gained during the time.

Pulling up at the barbershop, I grabbed my phone off the car charger before heading inside. As expected, it was jumping. From old to young, it was cats everywhere waiting on their turn to get in a chair. Good thing Ross, Dave's bro, owned the shop and looked out for family. I knew my wait wouldn't be long. Once I found a spot to have a seat, I pulled my phone out and begin to scroll through this iPhone that I'm still trying to figure all the way out. I mean, I got the basics of everything, but it's so many damn features and extra shit, making a nigga feel remedial as fuck.

"Nigga, what you over there focused on? I know you ain't hooked to that Book face bullshit already." Ross Questioned.

"What the hell is Book face?" Looking up from my phone, I questioned him back.

"Nigga, it's called Facebook." Another barber shouted out in laughter.

"Whatever the hell it's called. Yawl niggas knew what the fuck I meant." Ross said in his defense.

"Nah, I ain't on no social media. I just can't get into all that. Never been my cup of tea. Ain't bout to start now."

"Yeah. you say that shit now. Give it a few more months, they going have you sucked in and hooked too."

"Nah. I was locked up with too many niggas who got jammed up behind that social media shit. I don't want nothing tied to the government knowing all my business. I had enough of that during them six years. I'm coo."

"Yeah ight. You ready?" Ross said as his current client stood from his chair and checked himself over in the mirror.

"Just tighten me up. I know it ain't time for a cut just yet, but I gotta keep my lines fresh." I said as Ross placed the cape around my body.

Ross cleaned my line up, chopped a few words, and I headed to Polaris to grab a few items since I was north already. Polaris Mall seems so far but it's the only mall I can go to without running into half the bitches I used to fuck with before I got locked up. It's not like we got many shopping options in the city as it is. Easton is for sure a no go for me. Everybody and their grand momma be in that bitch like it's a chill spot or something.

As I browsed the racks of Saks, I felt my phone vibrating in my pocket. Pulling it out, I noticed Dave's name on the screen.

"Talk to me." I greeted him.

"Where your cool ass run off to?"

"Ha, I had to get up outta there before yawl started some shit I ain't want to be in the middle of."

"How did you know?" Dave joked.

"Soon as you told her it was time to roll, I knew something was about to come from nothing. Nyia might be a little older but that mouth ain't changed not one bit."

"Man, that stupid bitch complained the whole way to her crib. Then had the nerve to call me still talking shit after I got my whip from her crib and banged out."

"I thought you was blocking her ass?"

"You think I didn't. The bitch called too quick the first few times, but I'm in the clear now." We both started laughing cause we knew damn well he was only in the clear for so long.

"Enough of my gotdamn stressful ass day. Where you at? I'm trying to grab something to eat, but I'm tired of fucking fast food. I'm trying to take a trip to the Natti real quick for some Pappadeaux. I got a taste for got damn Alligator with some dirty rice."

"Who the fuck just wants some Alligator. I swear niggas get a little money and whole taste buds do a 180."

"I don't give a fuck what you talking bout is you down to ride or you ain't fuckin with it?"

"Nah I'll slide down there with you. I wanna stop by their outlet and see what it's hitting for."

"Bet, I'll meet you at the crib. Give me like fifteen minutes. I'm out south."

I ended the call and headed for the exit.

That nigga Dave and me been rocking since the sand box. The only nigga to never fold on me no matter the situation. Blood couldn't make us more family than what we already are. Once I got sentenced to that time it was an eye opener for the both of us. There was no other option besides for me to step away from the game, but Dave walked away voluntarily. That's when we decided it was time for us to start cleaning up the dirty money and do things the legal way so we both wouldn't end up behind bars.

Neoshi

Between pulling doubles and kicking it with Cassie's ass, I ain't been able to keep up on my sleep. No matter how hard I try to stay in the house, something won't allow me. Being home seems to depress me on a whole different type of level. I don't know if it's because I'm alone now or to blame it on Cassie.

For the past three years, I'd been in a serious relationship with a fuck nigga I thought was prince charming. When we broke up for the final time, I knew I had finally hit my breaking point with him and our relationship. Our final break up wasn't any different from our traditional on and off again break ups, but after so many years of bullshit, I just couldn't allow myself to go back. As much as I loved him that love started dying off more and more with every disagreement we had.

My way of healing and moving past my ex was burring myself in work and leisure to keep my mind occupied. I can't say that it was the most constructive thing to do but it damn sure was helping me past time until further notice. With Cassie being single, it only encouraged my behaviors. Only thing left for me to do is get some new outside dick and a bitch would be in the clear for the case of the EX.

"Bitch, I don't know how you convinced me to go anywhere with you after last night. I think I'm still drunk." Cassie complained as we walked into the True Religion store at the Cincinnati Premium Outlets.

"Your ass was throwing them back like you was a big dawg. Look at you now complaining." I joked with her.

"I don't know what the hell I was thinking killing two damn bottles of 1738 with you. Ain't no way in hell I should've drank that much liquor. Never have I and never will I again. I think I threw up maybe four times before I was able to even sleep good enough to get some of the drunkenness to wear off."

"See that's where you fucked up. I always pop me a fucking Zofran when I drink. Them little ass pills help like a muthafucka. They serve their purpose well in my life."

"Are you talking about them damn pills they prescribe for stomach virus and pregnant women's nausea?" Cassie looked at me confused.

"Hell yeah. Them bitches are heaven sent. I've never had a hangover since I got hip. You be thinking I'm playing when I say I'm bout to take my drinking pill, but I be dead ass serious."

"You damn right I thought you were playing. Who the fuck calls a prescription drug their drinking pill, when that's not what the hell it's prescribed for. You got a whole script of them?"

"Hell yeah. I got a couple of scripts for them things. I just keep them on hand for when I wanna get fucked up without the consequences. You better get your ass some too. I mean, what nurse works at a hospital and doesn't take full advantage of their resources available to them."

"A nurse who ain't trying to lose her license that's who." Cassie replied in a serious tone.

"Bitch please. I bet if your ass caught that shit you would get something to cure it without permission so don't go there with me.

"Yeah but that ain't about to happen so we don't even need to consider that situation."

"Whatever hoe." I said as I begin to browse the racks for some cheap shit."

After a good two hours of walking the outlets and shopping until our stomachs couldn't handle the hunger pains any longer, we both agreed on grabbing something to eat. Since we were in Cincinnati, we decided to stop by Pappadeaux. It had been a minute since we had some of their food. We used to come down at least twice a month, but it had been a good six months since I had some damn fried Alligator. My mouth was watering just thinking about it.

Thankful as hell the wait wasn't over twenty minutes when we arrived because I would've just had to order my shit to go otherwise, as our waitress showed us to our table, I started doing my happy dance. Cassie started laughing at me because she knew just how serious I got when it came to my food. I may have a little frame but better believe baby ain't missing out on any meals. Everything I eat always seems to go straight to my hips and butt anyhow. My top half of my body is small as hell including my breasts, but that ass though. That ass on a whole nother level.

The moment we sat down, I told the waitress I was ready to order my food. There was no need for small talk or for us to look over the menu. We already knew what we wanted and was very familiar with their selection to choose from. I order my fried Alligator with a side of red beans and rice. Cassie ordered her usual grilled Tilapia, jumbo shrimp and a side of gumbo. Neither one of us even thought about ordering any appetizers. Instead, I ordered me a drink to get my day started. Deciding against something strong, I picked something light and fruity. It was still kind of early in the day, and I wasn't trying to be drunk on the way back home and pass out on Cassie.

Our food didn't stand a chance leaving the restaurant. Wasn't nothing left to go in a to-go box, so we ordered desserts to go.

"Excuse me, I'm ok with getting a free meal and all but I ain't trying to get up and walk out for yawl to stop me cause I didn't pay." I said to the waitress as she placed our desserts on the table in bags ready to go.

"Oh, I'm sorry, the table over there with the two gentlemen already covered you ladies' tab." I looked at Cassie and smiled.

"Oh, well look at Gawd!" Cassie replied.

"Thank you!" I said and reached in my purse to see if I had some ones so I could at least tip her.

"It was nice of them to pay for our meal. One of them should've at least came over here and spoke." Cassie complained.

"Right. The nigga with the Rockstar jacket on kinda cute. I might just walk over there and speak, shit." I said as I looked over at the table with the two niggas and smiled.

"You and them damn light skin niggas. Your ass ain't goin learn. Them niggas is the devil." Cassie joked.

"I know right. A hard head makes a soft ass! Ayyeee!" I said with my tongue out.

"It took me one time, and I'm done. Bet the fuck I don't fuck with another light bright!" Cassie said before I turned to walk in the direction of the table with two gentlemen. I know Cassie ass probably looking at me like I'm cray but oh well. Closed mouths don't get fed.

"Excuse me, I'd like to thank you two on behalf of me and my friend's meal being covered." I said while eyeing the lighter of the two.

"Damn, took one of yawl long enough." The one I was eyeing replied, and I started laughing.

"Well actually, we just found out that you guys paid when she brought our dessert to our table. I didn't want to interrupt yawls meal or anything. Just wanted to show some gratitude." I said before turning to walk away while adding some extra umph to my switch.

Eyeing Cassie, I let a devilish grin spread across my face cause I knew exactly what I was doing. Cassie returned the devilish grin with a head nod and turned to head towards the exit. Before we could reach my car, I heard the same voice tone calling out after me. Pressing the unlock button on my keypad, I unlocked the doors so Cassie could get inside.

"Damn, you really gon' make a nigga run all the way to your car after you. I know you heard me yelling after you. Da fuck? A nigga just ate. I wasn't prepared to do no workout." He said as he pretended to catch his breath. I heard him but I didn't want him to know I was listening out for him.

"My fault sweetheart. I was talking to my girl. I didn't even hear you."

"Bullshit you ain't hear me. I ain't going for that. You gotta come up with something better." He said as he gave me the side-eye.

"I'm so serious." I giggled.

Dave

Going to Pappadeaux was a good idea. I wasn't expecting to run into some strange while there. Marco saw the shawty from last night he sent them drinks to. Of course it was his idea to cover their meal. I ain't complain cause it was coming out of that nigga pockets not mine. He can trick on that bitch all he wants, but if you ask me them drinks were more than enough. Especially considering she ain't gave up the ass yet.

When the chick who she was with walked over to our table and said thank you, my first thought was to shoot my shot then, but she walked away too quick. I wasn't going to confess that I didn't pay for their meal, so I took that as my opportunity to get in where I fit in. Shawty wasn't resistant though so it was a go for me. She gave me her number and I told her I would holler at her later in the evening. Marco wanted to act like a straight bitch talking bout once I smash the chick Neo then he will make his move on her homegirl. I told the nigga if I smash before he even gets ol girl's number I know the nigga done fell off on me.

Marco been out a good two, three months, and that nigga been focused on everything but pussy. I mean, don't get me wrong. I understand he want to make sure he got his priorities in line, but, brah! You gotta be shitting me. I ain't going a couple days with no pussy let alone anything longer. After doing a six-year bid, pussy would be the first thing on my agenda every day. I got arrested one fucking time and had to sleep in a cell for two days.

Those forty-eight hours felt like forty days and forty nights. Bet the fuck I don't ever do that shit again, especially not voluntarily.

"Nigga you driving like it's NASCAR. Slow the fuck down. We ain't in no rush." Marco complained from the passenger side of my 2018 Suburban.

"Fuck you talkin bout. I'm only going seventy nigga. What you want me to do? Slow down and drive Miss Daisy?"

"Ain't no way in hell you going no fuckin seventy nigga."

"Nigga sit back, relax and enjoy the ride." I said before turning the music back up. I had to tune that nigga out. I wasn't bout to let his paranoia fuck up my vibe.

By the time we got back to the city, it was time to run to the crib, freshen up and step out on the scene for day two of my nigga's welcome home celebration weekend. Marco didn't want no welcome home party or gathering, so I planned to get a section everyday of the weekend and just turn up that way. At first, it didn't make sense to me why the nigga kept refusing to have one big ass kickback, but when he explained his reasoning I felt where he was coming from.

The nigga Marco cut off every fucking body who wrote him off when he got locked up. The nigga didn't fuck with a soul besides me and Ross. I couldn't blame him, though. Niggas turned snakes or fakes when them charges came back. Although it ain't a nigga's responsibility to take care of another man or hold him down when he gets locked up, loyalty should automatically make you make sure your dawg good behind them bars.

Niggas ain't cut like they used to be though. It's like we the last ones left of a rare breed. The bitches Marco used to fuck with before his bid, he wouldn't even do a double look at. I thought the nigga was just capping until we ran into a bitch name Dina he used to fuck with back in the day. I never thought the nigga would stop fucking around with her, but he proved me wrong.

Dina always been cold but the bitch cocaine crazy. I knew for sure she was going to ride it out with my dawg, and he was going change the hoe last name once he touched down, but man was wrong. That bitch was on the next nigga pole before Marco got shipped out to the county jail. What bitches fail to realize is, no matter how sneaky they are, niggas behind bars find out information quicker than the streets do. Marco told me some nigga she was fucking on little brother was locked up with him and all Dina's secrets were out the bag. Marco played it smooth like he ain't give a fuck, but I know the nigga was hurt deep down.

Don't nothing fuck up a nigga pride more than been shitted on at his low points. That hurt turn to anger real quick when you in a fucked-up situation. I guess Dina thought the nigga Marco was just bullshitting by not trying to fuck with her before he came home. When she approached us in the mall I wanted to run and hide for her. Marco tried to ignore the hoe, but she came up to us being all loud like she belonged on one of our arms. That nigga shut that shit down in the middle of the mall in front of everybody passing. The bitch had tears running down her face by the time I got my phone out my pocket to record the shit. Yeah, I was going record the shit, oh well. I'm just that type of nigga. I needed something to look back on and laugh about.

Instead of having a flock of niggas with us like we did last night, it was only Marco, Dave and me stepping out tonight. To make sure the same fuck shit ain't happened as last night I made sure I rode with Dave and Marco. Wasn't no way I was getting set up for Nyia bullshit this time. Once we got inside of club Drip, we headed straight to the VIP section. It's not that we too good to chill in the crowd with everyone else, but niggas get to acting corny and I'll fuck a nigga up over my shoes being stepped on cause I'm just that petty.

"Nigga, don't order more than three bottles tonight. I'm taking it slow." Marco said when he took a seat on the white two-seater couch.

"I don't give a fuck what you taking nigga. I'm getting fucked up. My muthafuckin brotha home nigga!" I screamed to no one in particular. My plan was to go hard all weekend. I don't know what the fuck Marco was thinking but we bout to get fucked up. I don't care how slow he planned on taking it.

Shortly after the bottle girls returned with our bottles, I eyed a shawty on the dance floor that resembled the chick from Pappadeaux, but I wasn't sure. I had forgotten all about getting at her, but I made a mental note to shoot her a text before I got too fucked up tonight.

Ain't nobody freak like me

Give ya what you need like me

Ain't nobody got on they tip, tip toes and rode to the tip like me

Got em addicted, he feigning

Megan Thee Stallion "Big Ole Freak" had the bitches showing out all over the club. If a nigga ain't know any better, I would've thought all them bitches bouncing they booty to the beat could do that shit they rocking to. That's never the case though; a bitch will dance her ass off on the dance floor but get home and can't ride the dick to save her life. Homegirl Meg for damn sure got a bunch of hoes out here false advertising and shit.

Marco

For me to keep running into this same girl, it had to be a sign. Two days in a row at three different locations wasn't just no coincidence type of occurrence. Instead of paying for her drink or her food again, I decided I was going to approach shawty and see what's up. After all the bitches got their twerk on and feet were good and tired, I made my move to the bar area where I saw her sitting.

"Excuse me miss. Can I talk to you for a second?" I asked as I approached her.

"Yeah, that's fine." She said before bringing her cup to her lips to take a sip. Watching her take a sip from her straw did something to me. That little ass gesture had a nigga damn near rocked up.

"You here alone or you wit ya man?" I wanted to make sure she was available before I went any further with our conversation.

"Neither." She replied with a smirk on her face.

"So, who you here with if you don't mind me asking."

"Nah, I don't mind. I'm here with my girls. Who you here with?"

"My brothas."

"Oh ok. If I'm not mistaken, you're the guy from the restaurant earlier aren't you. You and your friend covered me and my girl's tab. Thank you for that by the way." I low-key felt some type of way that she recognized me from earlier but was still playing it smooth like she ain't know a nigga was interested in her.

"Yeah that's me. It's no problem though. I figured since I didn't introduce myself earlier why not do so now. I'm Marco, what's your name?"

"Nice to meet you, Marco. I'm Casanae." She said as she reached her hand out to shake my hand.

"Nice to meet you, too, Casanae. So, you single or you taken before I waste time."

"I'm single. How about yourself?"

"Single as a dolla bill baby. Can I take you to lunch or dinner sometime?" I couldn't think of shit else to say to her besides offering to take her out at a later date.

"That doesn't sound like a bad idea. She said and gave me a seductive smile before taking another sip of her drink.

Casanae gave me her number and I headed back to the VIP section. When I got back to my seat Dave goofy ass was waiting to see if I made my move like he was watching me from afar or some shit.

Before we dropped Ross off at his crib, we slid by the Waffle House to grab something to eat. That bitch was jumping like it was the club. You would think it would be played out by now, but I guess some niggas never change. Niggas was flocking up at the Waffle House after the club before I got locked up; that shit should be played out by now. Picking up some food to go home should be the only thing a nigga pulling up for. Ain't no social hour at 3 o'clock in the morning.

I fucked that All Star meal up; it was just what I needed after two days of drinking. I knew it would've been even better had I ate the shit last night when I got it. The moment we go to the crib, I passed out. I didn't even realize I was that fucked up until my body hit the bed. Next thing I knew, I was waking up to Dave stupid ass singing in the shower. I swear that nigga has been fried since birth.

"Last night, Last night!" Dave said with a goofy ass grin on his face as he flopped down on the couch.

"What about last night?" I questioned while taking a sip from my bottle of Dasani water.

"I ain't goin lie, I got some cuddy last night!" Dave said imitating the movie ATL.

"You's a got damn lie. You ain't get no cuddy last night". I laughed and replied.

"Like hell I did!"

"Let me guess, Nyia gave in and gave you some pussy last night?"

"Hell Nah. That bitch still on my block list as we speak. You thought I was playing. I was dead ass. I'm not bout to play with

Nyia man. I was inside some new walls last night! I felt like a nigga was in the escape room or something and them walls was caving in on me. Had to be the Henny fucking with my mind." Dave joked.

"When this shit happen?" I questioned because I clearly remembered Dave and I coming back to the crib together. I ain't hear the alarm go off last night indicating that someone had come in or went out. Then again, I did pass out so who knows.

"Shortly after we got home, I dipped back out. I met up with ol girl Neoshi."

"WHO?" I replied with my face frowned up. I had never heard that name a day in my life.

"You know ol girl's friend. The chick from OT. The chick who friends with that bitch you low key stalking."

"Fuck outta here. I ain't stalking shit." I laughed "How that shit ends up happening?"

"I shot her a text when we were at Drip. We went back and forth while we were there, and I guess her drinks had her on some freaky shit cause it went down last night."

"You went to her crib?"

"Nah, we met up at a room. Fuck I look like going to that bitch house. I don't know that hoe like that. She wasn't bout to set me up on some drunk shit slippin."

"Damn, all this happened while I was passed out cold. That's why your ass was in the shower acting like Jon B and shit singing all early."

"Aww, here you go with the light skin nigga jokes." Dave said and headed to the kitchen. This nigga stays talking shit but soon as somebody joke about him in comparison to a light skin nigga he want to get serious.

I grabbed my phone and decided to send Casanae a quick text to see if she was free to have lunch or dinner with me today. Dave planned on kicking it all weekend but today being Sunday I was ready to just relax and prepare for my week ahead. Besides, it's not like I just came home; it's going on three months and this weekend was the first time I actually went out to a bar or club. Honestly, I can't even say it's my thing anymore. The crowds and the hype ain't what it used to be to me no more. Now that I have experienced it again, I can say I wasn't missing out on nothing by not going out kicking it on the regular basis.

To my surprise, Casanae didn't play hard to get or take forever to respond to any of my texts. She seemed pretty coo so far. She agreed to have dinner with me at Ruth Chris later for dinner and sent me her address to pick her up. Instead of looking like a thirsty ass nigga and texting her all day until our little meet-up or date, whatever you want to call it, I decided to stop texting and save the rest of my conversation for dinner time.

Casanae

When Marco texted me earlier today, I was kind of surprised. Normally niggas talk a good game in the bar or club when they drunk bout taking you out but, in actuality, they just want to take you home after the club. Not him; he didn't even contact me until after noon today and one of the first questions he asked me was had I ate and how was I feeling. My first mind was to blow him off because of course I was hung over, but something told me to stop running from niggas and give him a chance.

It's not that I have being running from every guy that tried to talk to me, but I wasn't rushing into talking to anyone. It seems like everyone starts off the same and seem oh so perfect then BOOM, here come some bullshit. I'm content with not listening to anyone's lies and being played around with so I just been kicking it living my single life without any complaints. I guess a little friendly dinner wouldn't hurt; it's been a minute anyways since I been out on a date.

Ruth Chris is a nice restaurant but nothing extremely fancy where I'm required to dress up, so I decided to keep it casual. The True Religion curvy skinny jeans that I picked up from the outlet the other day fit perfectly with the off the shoulder happy hour black bodysuit I ordered from Fashion Nova months ago. The black ankle booties set my entire outfit off. I wasn't too dressy nor too casual. My sleek, extended ponytail was still in place thanks to me tying my hair up last night. I'm not a big fan of make-up so just a coat of clear MAC gloss was enough for me. After looking myself over for what felt like the tenth time, I decided to go have a shot to calm my nerves.

I don't know why the closer it got to the time for Marco to pick me up the more nervous I got. Pacing the damn floor and looking in the mirror to make sure nothing was out of place was going to have me a fucking wreck before he arrived. Instead of taking one shot, I decided on a double of Hennessy. Soon as I placed the bottle of Hennessey back on counter, my phone text notifications went off. Rushing to my phone in the living room, I looked at my watch before checking my message; it was seven-thirty on the dot.

Neoshi: Have fun bish and get me some shrimp to go. Thanks, MUAH!

ME: LMAO, who told you I was taking a to-go box when we left.

Neoshi: Bitch, come on. I got a taste for their shrimp the moment you said yawl was going there. Don't do your bestie like that.

ME: Whatever hoe. I'll text or call you when I'm headed home so you can come pick up your damn shrimp.

As I pressed send on the last message to Neoshi, I heard a knock on my door. I knew it had to be Marco because I wasn't expecting any other company. Looking myself over once more in the full-length mirror in the corner of my living room, I made sure everything was in place. I still made sure to check the peephole before opening the door, and like expected, it was Marco.

"Hey." I greeted him.

"Hey Miss Lady. You ready?" He questioned.

"Yeah, let me grab my clutch and my keys." I said before turning to the stand to grab my items.

Marco walked maybe a foot behind me as he walked me to his car and even opened the car door for me like a real gentleman. When I got into the passenger side of his Navy-Blue Audi, I was pleased. Many young guys try to be extremely flashy with Chargers, Challengers, and so forth but Audi's scream grown man shit all day if you ask me. I wasn't sure what year it was, but I know all the gadgets inside were digital and a lot newer than the features in my 2016 Toyota Camry.

Just as he opened the door for me when he picked me up, he also pulled up to valet and opened the door for me when we arrived at the restaurant. Every door he opened and allowed me to walk through first. Once we were inside of the restaurant, he stood next to me and, when the hostess addressed us, he spoke up first and told her his name for his reservation he had set for us. The initiative he took for this date so far was receiving mental brownie points.

Upon sitting down at the table we were escorted to, Marco pulled my chair our for me and then took his seat. Sitting across from him at the table I was able to observe all of his facial features that weren't as visible in the club nor from afar when I saw him out of town. Marco was even more sexy than I originally gave him credit for. His skin tone was almost the perfect brown if that even existed, strong facial features, a clean-cut fade, full goatee, and dark brown eyes, with straight, white teeth.

Our conversation during dinner seemed to flow as if we had known each other longer than 24 hours. I discovered that Marco was fresh home from the federal prison, which I would've never guessed. Most men who been locked up are covered in tattoos and look like street niggas, but not Marco. I mean, he doesn't rub me as the square type of dude based off his demeanor alone. I could tell he's been around the block before. His conversation and the way he carries himself is what caused me to be surprised by his past. I declined on asking questions about what led him to prison. Instead, I'll wait until a later date to find that information out.

Marco told me that he was partners with his friend Dave. They owned several car washes and laundry mats throughout the city. It was good to know he wasn't slanging dope across the city, and I wouldn't be in jeopardy of being arrested from being in the company of him. Over dinner, I learned that he wasn't the guy his image portrays. I know I have a type whether I admit it or not, which is why I keep ending up single. Obviously, my type isn't what's best for me. The thuggish demeanor has always been the type I fall for and Marco does fit that physical description but only time will tell if he's the same as the others. Let's hope for the both of our sake that not judging a book by its cover will be my theory with him.

Our entire dinner date was a success, from our meal selections, to our conversation. The date went so well I honestly didn't want it to end. Considering it had been so long since I enjoyed the company of man, it was overdue. Marco had so much going for him, including the fact that he didn't have any children. I definitely could see us having a part two to our date night.

Riding back to my place we rode damn near in silence just vibing to old skoo music. Marco didn't rub me as the slow jam type of guy, but I was feeling his playlist for sure.

"I enjoyed dinner with you." Marco said as he pulled up in front of my place.

"I enjoyed our date, too, if that's what you wanna call it." I replied with a giggle.

"Yeah, I guess you can call it a date. I ain't got no problem with that. What's your plans for the rest of your evening?"

"My evening is over with. I have work in the morning, so I'm about to go in here and get my stuff ready for tomorrow. I have a double shift to pull so I'll be in bed right after that. I did enough this weekend." I replied.

"You and me both. Well I don't have to work a double, but I did enough for the weekend."

"What are you about to do then?"

"I'm heading home. Probably find something to watch on firestick and crash."

"Sounds relaxing."

"So, is this going to be the last time I get face to face time with you or can we do this again soon?" I was waiting for him to ask to see me again, but I didn't want to answer too quick. Mentally, I was already picking out my outfit for our next date but he ain't need to know that.

"No not at all. We can for sure meet up again. How soon are you talking?"

"Well I don't know your schedule but whenever you're free is ok with me. I don't do too much of nothing. I take care of my business and lay low for the most part, but I could use some company when I'm not conducting business."

"Ok, well we'll come up with something. I don't know my schedule for the remainder of the week, only tomorrow, Tuesday and Wednesday for sure are twelve-hour shifts for me."

"Alright bet. I'm not going to hold you much longer since I know you got a long day ahead of you tomorrow." Marco said before he got out the car and headed around to the passenger side to open the door for me.

He walked me to the door and even gave me a nice tight hug before he walked away. I made sure to inhale whatever fragrance he had on before he walked away. Gawd that man smelled good enough to eat.

Soon as I locked the door behind me, I called Neo to tell her come pick up these funky ass shrimps she had me order before I forgot. Not wanting to text Marco first, I busied myself with preparing my work stuff for the week.

Neoshi

I wasn't expecting to give up the goodies the first night I kicked it with Dave but shit YOLO. Good thing the dick was good cause I would've been salty I gave it up that quick if he was wack. After that night, I knew for sure I was ready for the world and to live my best life and prepare for my hot girl summer. Fucking something new was the last step to getting the hell over my last relationship. Good dick will have you like ex-nigga who; that bad shit may have caused me to run my ass back where I don't belong.

Dave coo but I ain't looking for a relationship or anything remotely close to one. He never said he was either so right now we on the same page. After I fucked him on the first night, I didn't see no point in trying to hold out on him or wait until the next time so needless to say I doubled back a few times since the first encounter. It's only been a couple of weeks since the first time but I lost count fa real on how many times we actually fucked.

Casanae and Marco had started linking and talking on the phone as well, but she hadn't given up the goodies yet. Like Cassie and I, Marco and Dave are complete opposites as well. Cassie is the calm one out of the two of us, just as Marco is the laid back of them two. Marco is trying to wine and dine my bestie and Dave over here beating my damn guts every chance he can.

"I don't know why you in here laying down like shit sweet. Toot that thing up. I'm ready for round two." Dave said as he walked into his bedroom where I was laid out across his bed in only my birthday suit.

"How was I supposed to know you was ready for another round. You the one complained your leg caught a damn cramp." I joked with him.

"Just cause my leg cramped don't mean my dick don't work. We just going to have to switch it up. Come toot that little shit up over here." Dave instructed for me to come to the edge of the bed so he could hit it from the back.

"Now you know this shit ain't little. Don't play with me." I said as I slapped my ass so he could see it jiggle before I bent over the footboard of the bed.

As Dave placed his left hand on the arch of my back, I felt him ease the tip inside of me and pull it back out slowly. After slowly easing in and out of me a few times, he quickened his pace and force with each thrust. Each pump was more forceful than the last, causing my titties to slap my stomach at a rapid pace.

Pounding me from the back while occasionally slapping my ass for extra excitement had a bitch full of bliss. Originally, I told myself I wouldn't be moaning all loud and shit because we didn't know when Marco would be back home, but I couldn't hold it in any longer. My moans were getting louder and louder by the minute. The louder my moans got, the wetter my pussy got and the harder he fucked me.

"Damn Neo. This some good ass pussy! Make a nigga wanna sing to it." Dave grunted. Even during sex he's a fucking comedian.

"Sing to it then baby!" I said in between moans.

"Ahhh. Ummm. Shit what you want me to sing?" I couldn't do anything besides laugh. This nigga really had the nerve to ask me what I wanted him to sing in the middle of us fucking. "Stop being lazy, throw that pussy back at me. I'mma catch it every trip, don't even worry."

Instead of saying anything back, I followed his orders and started matching his pace and thrust. With every pump, I matched him.

"Dave… Dave I'm bout to cum." I moan loudly as I felt the chills run through my entire body.

"What you waiting on then baby. Cum for me." Just like that, I came on demand for him.

"FUUUUUCCKKK!" Dave grunted loudly as he pulled his dick from inside of me and nutted all over my ass.

"Go see if Marco came back yet, so I can run and hop in the shower." I told Dave.

"That nigga ain't coming home no time soon. Take your ass in there and get in the shower so I can finish you off in there."

"NO! No, we done for the day!" I protested.

"No? Did she just tell us NO?" Dave looked down at his dick as if he was waiting on a response.

"Move boy, you better go on somewhere." I said as I brushed past him with one of his oversized t shirts on and my clothes in hand.

"BOY? Did she just call me a boy?" Dave yelled out still talking to his dick, and I closed the bathroom door behind me ignoring his comments. Although I told Dave No I knew for a fact once he heard the water on for a couple of minutes he was going to bust in the bathroom and join me.

As I lathered the soap onto my wash rag, I heard the door open, and just as I thought, Dave was heading in for more. I looked over at him and simply shook my head. There was nothing more I could do because I knew he was going to pull this stunt. Thank goodness I didn't have any plans after this cause this nigga was going to have me out of commission for the day. Too many dick thrashings in one day will have my ass stuck in bed on chill for the rest of the day.

"Scoot your ass up. I ain't trying to get scalded by that hot ass water." Dave said causing me to bust out into laughter as he squeezed into the shower behind me.

"Shut up; the water ain't even that hot. You just be complaining. If you don't like my water temperature stop trying to shower with me and wait your turn."

"Shit if I do wait a turn, and this my fucking shower. Bet I get in and get some more of this ass while I'm in here." Dave said as he gripped my hips and eased in me from behind. Just like that, we were back at it for another round of Dave pleasureful comedy show, just the shower edition this time.

Dave

Neoshi wasn't gone a good fifteen minutes before I heard somebody banging on the front door. Thinking it was Neoshi's ass coming back because she forgot something, I ran to the door with just my boxers on without looking out the peephole. Swinging the door open, imagine my face when I seen it was Nyia ass standing there with her hand on her hip, holding my son's arm with her free hand.

"Why the fuck you ain't answering none of my calls?" Nyia started her shit as she pushed passed me into the house.

Of course, I closed the door behind her because I wasn't trying to have my neighbors in my business. And I for damn sure wasn't trying to have Neoshi circle the block and see me standing in the door in some fucking draws talking to my baby mom. That shit wouldn't look good from any angle.

"HELLO? You don't fucking hear me?" Nyia yelled in my direction. I damn sure didn't hear a word she said. I was too caught off guard by her popping up on my ass.

"Nyia, don't start that shit today, man."

"What you mean don't start that shit today? That's you. I try to be cordial with you and "coparent" as you call it. But no, you just can't seem to get the concept of the whole idea you suggested."

"Fuck do you mean I can't grasp the concept. I take care of my fucking son so miss me with that shit." This bitch always wanna argue; that's why we ain't together now.

"You financially take care of him. That's what the fuck you do. Nothing more nothing less. I called you fucking twelve times; it could've been an emergency or anything, but did you check to see? NO, you fucking didn't."

"Ok, and you act like you calling twelve times is something new. You do that type of shit when you bored, too, so I'm supposed to know it was important this time around. Yeah, Ok!"

"Either way it goes, I have your one and only fucking child. Every time I call, you should answer. You never know what it could be. Every time you call, I answer. It don't matter if it's one in the afternoon or one in the morning, I answer. So why is it so hard for you to do the same?"

"When the last time I called your funky ass at one in the morning? Don't get quiet now."

"Just the other fucking day when you wanted me to suck your sweaty ass dick after you left the club, or did you forget?"

"That shit was damn near a month ago. Try again, my friend."

"Yesterday, last week, either way you did it."

"Ok Nyia. Enough of the extra bullshit. What you come all the way over here for? My son looks ok to me so what's the problem, or should I say what's the emergency."

"Ain't no emergency with him. You're right; he is fine, but that's no thanks to you. I called cause the Sheriff came and put a note on my door for me to move out within forty-eight hours. Me and DJ need to come stay here." My eyes damn near popped out my fucking head like we were in some sort of cartoon.

"What?! What you mean they put a paper on your door for you to get out in two days? How that supposed to work? Why they put a paper on your door? You ain't paying your fucking rent but you stay buying that stiff ass weave every chance you get."

"First of all, my weave ain't fucking stiff. Secondly, I did pay my fucking rent dummy. My landlord defaulted on their loan without letting me know so basically, it's not his house anymore; it belongs to the bank. We already got another place to move into, but I can't move in just yet cause it's not ready." My mind started wandering like a muthafucka. Nyia and me under one roof ain't a good combination.

"Ok, so when your other place going be ready? You can't call and let them know your situation so they can speed up the process?" I questioned her and she only shook her head and appeared to be irritated that I even asked that question.

"No, they can't. So, me and DJ need to come here until it is." Nyia said and looked at me as if she dared me to protest what she was saying.

Instead of continuing to argue with her I just agreed so she could get the fuck out my face for the moment. I had a lot of shit to work out before her and my son could just come stay with me. My son would never be a problem, but Nyia, on the other hand, would be. It's not like I lived in the house alone. Marco is my roommate, and I got to respect his opinion on this situation as well. I mean I know he would never turn my son away, but this was still something I should've run past him before agreeing to it first.

I ain't have no intentions on stepping out tonight but a drink on the couch just wasn't going to cut it.

Drip was for sure popping for it to be a Tuesday. I didn't expect the crowd to be this heavy. Had I known that, I would've got dressed instead of throwing on some damn old ass sweatpants and a tee shirt. Bitches was out like it was lady's night in their finest attire.

I sat at the bar and had a few drinks while I waited on my food to be done. One drink turned into bout six of them bitches. Before I knew it, a nigga was drunk and thinking about Neoshi ass. I could for sure use some pussy at a time like this to ease my nerves.

Just thinking about how the fuck I was going to work my life around Nyia and DJ living with me caused me to have another drink. How the fuck I'm gon' sound saying my baby mom moved in with me but we not fuckin or together. Who the fuck really gon' believe that shit? I half want to believe I ain't gon' fuck the bitch while she living in my house. I mean, that's in-house pussy. Pussy on demand. How the hell I'm supposed to turn that down? I'm a freaky type of nigga, and I love to fuck, bottom line.

My phone started vibrating in my pocket taking me away from my drink and thoughts. When I pulled the phone from my pocket, I saw that it was Marco calling. That only stressed me out even more. I still hadn't even talked to him about this whole situation. I declined the call and sent him a text letting him know I was at Drip, but I would be to the crib in bout twenty mins.

Nyia

I don't know what Dave's problem is. It's like one minute we get along just fine and the next minute we at each other's necks like fucking enemies. Dave and I been on and off for damn near ten years. You would think we would have it together by now, but we just can't get shit right. I thought after knowing him for so long and dealing with him, the birth of our first child would seal the deal for us, but it didn't. It seems like after I had DJ, things only got worse between us.

Now don't take what I said out of context. I'm not saying I thought me having DJ would lock Dave down. I know a kid won't keep no man. What I'm saying is, after so many years with a person, the only thing left to do is get married and have children. Since marriage wasn't the first step for us, I won't lie and say I didn't think it would come shortly after the baby. Boy was I wrong, we barely talk half the time, let alone a ring.

When I went over Dave's house two days ago, I blew the entire situation of me moving up to make it sound a lot worse than it was. The Sheriff did put a sticker on my door, but it wasn't when I told him. They had *been* put it on there. I knew if I told Dave that, he would ask why I waited until the last minute. Truth is I hadn't even looked for another place yet. I didn't see no point in rushing to move into a new place until Dave and me had something figured out between the two of us. My section eight voucher can be on hold for up to six months before they take it.

My plan is to start looking for a new place for the three of us to move in around month four.

When we broke up the last time and Dave moved out of my house, we originally agreed to take some time apart. Like, a little break for us both to work on ourselves, but we weren't working on a damn thing besides each other's nerves right about now. Dave doesn't even seem to be putting forth any effort. Especially now since Marco is home; it seems like he's even more resistant to be a family man. I understand Marco was away for a nice amount of time, but Marco is his nigga and just that. Me and DJ are Dave's family he created which should be his number one priority.

I don't have nothing against Marco, but he doesn't have the same responsibilities as Dave. Marco is a bachelor with no damn kids or a long-term woman so he can live the free life, but Dave,, on the other hand needs to man up and stop trying to rip and run the streets like he's still a fuckin kid.

"You better get the fuck up off your ass and carry some of these damn boxes before they be left for the got damn Sheriff to keep." Dave fussed as he walked out the house carrying boxes from DJ's room.

"Nigga, I'm tired. I need a five-minute break." I complained.

"Tired my ass." He yelled back into the house.

Instead of continuing my little break from moving, I got up and grabbed the smallest box I could find and headed outside to the U-Haul. Dave, Ross, and Marco had moved damn near my entire house into the U-Haul and to the storage unit. The most I did was pack everything into boxes. Most of my stuff would be going into storage because Dave's house was already fully furnished. Besides, he claimed the more stuff I brought, the longer I would try to stay.

Dave didn't have no problem letting me know this was a temporary thing. Little did he know I had a plan for us move out together. Not just me and our son alone without him. I've been trying my hardest not to slip up and mention anything about my future plans for us until after about a month or so.

Once everything was moved into the storage and out of my house, we headed to Dave's. When we arrived, Dave made sure I heard him loud and clear when he said I am to park in front of their house and not in the driveway. As bad as I wanted to protest, considering I have the baby, I didn't.

When I walked into the house, I was a little taken back when Dave told me all my shit was in the basement. Like why wouldn't my shit be in his bedroom.

"Why is my shit down here in the basement when you have a room upstairs?" I questioned with attitude in my tone.

"Where your shit gon' fit in my room if I already got all my shit in there. Think about it!" Dave replied while still moving my boxes around so we could have a walkway.

"Oh, ok so. Well that box right there can go upstairs to your room, oh and this one too." I said pushing the boxes that were labeled for my clothing.

"For what?" Dave looked at me as if I grew two heads.

"Ahh, so they can be put away. Ain't that what closets made for." I replied while looking at him as if that was a stupid ass question for him to ask.

"Well, my closet was made for MY clothes to go in NOT yours."

"So, you really expect me to come down here everyday to go through boxes to find my clothes when you can just make room for some of my clothes."

"What you mean come down here every day? This where you gon' be. You can roll over and get your clothes, skip to get your clothes, run to get your clothes, shit you might even have enough space to do cartwheels to get your clothes. I don't care how you get them, that's on you."

"Here you go playing. Dave, I'm tired. I don't feel like playing with you tonight. Can you just take that box upstairs so I can get JR in the bath and lay down?"

"Ain't nobody playing. I'm dead ass; this is your space until your place is ready. This whole basement. You got your own bathroom and everything. You got your space, and I got mine."

"Wait, so you seriously think me and your son bout to sleep in the basement of your house while you sleep upstairs in your bedroom? How does that sound? That don't even make sense." This nigga must've lost his damn mind.

"My son can sleep upstairs with me, but you... you, my friend, have to sleep down here. No, you can not sleep, lay or lounge around in my bedroom. And what you mean how that sound? It sounds like a plan to me. A smart plan if you ask me."

"Dave, I'm not bout to argue with you. This shit is stupid as fuck. Like, I don't know what the fuck type of logic in your head."

"Shit, you asked could yawl stay here until your crib was ready. You have your own space and everything, what fucking more do you want? The basement is fully furnished and it's finished. Besides, you ain't paying not one fucking bill so what the fuck is you complaining for? You ain't my woman. Why would you even think it was coo for us to be shacking up like some happy ass couple when we not." Dave's phone started to ring, and he silenced the call only pissing me off even more.

"Why you silence your phone? You don't want your little bitches to hear me in the background when you answer." I yelled.

"My phone ain't none of your business. Whether I answer my phone or silence it ain't got shit to do with you being in the background. I'm busy right now. All that yelling shit you gon' have to chill on. It ain't only us living here. Be respectful to Marco. This his house, too; you're a fucking Guest. You hear me? A fucking guest. Get that shit through your head and be grateful." Dave said and headed upstairs with DJ on his trail.

The fact that Dave was treating me like I was some chick he just met and not the mother of his child hurt. The tears in my eyes were not only from the pain I felt in my heart but the rage I felt too. I wanted to run upstairs after him and fuck his ass up, but I knew that would only lead to a big ass fight and me being put the fuck out tonight. I got something for his ass. I'm going to sleep down here in the basement tonight, but this will not be where I lay my head every night I'm here.

Marco

Man, When I tell you the past two weeks been awkward as hell, I mean that. Having Nyia living at the crib just feel weird as fuck. She lucky she got nephew, or she would've been assed out. I don't give two fucks about the history her and Dave got. Living in a house with your nigga, his baby mom, and they child just ain't what I imagined when I got out of jail.

Dave was going through it even more than me, cause it's his baby mom. That nigga done turned into a straight alchy. All he does is drink from the time he wake up until he lay down. He said that's the only way he can refrain from putting his hands on her. Nyia be talking her shit so I feel where he coming from. She ain't changed none from before I left. Still full of drama and childish ass behaviors. I notice when she realizes I'm home or around she pipes down some, but it be too late.

Originally, I thought Nyia and Dave were going to share his room, but that nigga was adamant about her staying in the basement. I thought by now he would've given in, or at least had a drunk night but he hadn't. Dave barely home anymore. Well, that makes the both of us. During the week, I'm handling stuff with our businesses, and on the weekends, I been with Casanae.

Whenever she free, I try to get in where I fit in. Casanae is the total package, and I enjoy her company. She not like a lot of women my age. Casanae got a good head on her shoulders and is about her business. Damn near thirty with no kids, she's a nurse, her own condo, intellectual conversations, pretty face and a banging ass body. From my point of view, she's not lacking in any area.

"I'm hungry as fuck. What you bout to eat?" Dave questioned as he walked into my office in the back of our main laundry mat.

"When you get here?" I questioned him.

"I just got here. I had to find somewhere to go. It ain't like I can go home and have some peace. That bitch getting on my last fucking nerves. I'm ready to call around and see if somebody got a place ready she can move into NOW!"

"Your fried. What she do now?" I laughed.

"What she ain't do is the question. I'm tired of seeing her fucking face. I'm sick of hearing her voice. Shit, I'm tired of sharing the same damn air with this bitch. I thought for sure there was no way I could hate her any more than I already did but I do now." Dave said as he took a seat at my desk across from me.

"Not the same air. You wildin nigga."

"Nah, fa real. She wake up talking shit. She always got something to complain about or give her two cents on. Like bitch, just shut the fuck up. Don't nobody want to hear her voice every got damn day."

"I'm surprised you ain't used to her by now."

"Ain't no getting used to that."

"After twenty years of being around and with a person you would think you would." I came back.

"I don't give a fuck if I knew her and was married to her since I came out that nigga sack. I could NEVER get used to that shit."

"I mean, I don't know that side of her. I only know what you tell me and what I see."

"That should be enough."

"Did she tell you when she was moving yet? Yawl gon' have to hire Two Men and a Truck this time. I ain't moving all that bullshit again."

"Hell no. Every time I ask the dumb bitch what the people say about her place, she starts a fucking argument. And nigga you ain't said shit. I already told her she gotta find some movers. I ain't no hard labor ass nigga. We ain't carry our own furniture in the crib. Fuck I look like doing it again for her?"

"Where she moving to anyways?" I was hoping like hell it wasn't nowhere near where we lived."

"She won't fucking tell me, like it's classified information. I told you she keeps picking arguments. I'm starting to think she ain't got no place. She keeps playing I'm gon' fuck around and call her messy ass sister and pay her to find out for me." I damn near fell out my chair laughing at the shit this nigga said.

"You laughing but still ain't answer the question I asked when I walked in this bitch. WHAT the fuck we gon' eat? I'm fuckin starved."

"Nyia been cooking damn near every day. I was gon' wait to see what she whipped up at the crib before I decided if I was gon' go grab something or not."

"You on your own there, Big Dawg. I ain't eating shit else she cook. That bitch probably gon' try to put some voodoo on me or poison my shit. Plus, the bitch can't cook that good no way. That shit be basic. Shit, she basic! That's it. Nyia is a mediocre ass bitch. Maybe that's why I can't fuck wit her on that level no more."

"You just now realizing this?" I joked while laughing.

"Fuck you. I'm bout to go grab Neoshi and get something to eat. I'll catch up with you later." Dave said before exiting my office.

On the real, I felt sorry for my brotha. Dave was in between a rock and hard place. Either put Nyia and their son out or deal with it. It's not that he would put nephew out but Nyia wouldn't think twice about taking DJ if Dave put her out. Nephew the only thing she got to hold over Dave head. Without him Dave wouldn't have no reason to deal with her.

I wasn't even thinking about eating, now my stomach got the nerve to be growling all loud. Might as well hit up Casanae and see if she wanted to grab something to eat with me.

Me: What's up beautiful?

Casanae: Hey handsome!

Me: What you doin? You ate?

Casanae: Nothing, just got off work. I ate earlier but not dinner yet.

Me: You ready to eat dinner or you wanna wait?

Casanae: I could eat now. Let me get in the shower and outta these work clothes.

Me: Bet, I'm gon' leave the laundry mat in like thirty minutes.

Casanae: Ok that's fine.

Casanae

I enjoy the fact that Marco like to take me out and spend time, but I hate that we always have to go out to eat. Sometimes I just wanna sit at home and eat a nice cooked meal. If I ain't know any better, I would think the nigga is trying to get me fat. Every time I talk to him one of the first questions is have you ate. Sometimes I tell him I have just so it doesn't look like I'm waiting or expecting him to feed me every day.

"You wanna eat here or grab it to go?" Marco questioned as we looked around at the crowd of people in the lobby of P. F. Chang's.

"We can just get it to go. It honestly doesn't matter to me; it's up to you." I replied.

"Coo, we can take it to go." Marco said before he grabbed a menu for us to look over so we could decide exactly what we wanted to eat.

The wait for our food was just as long as if we were dining in but I didn't complain. Marco ordered Miso Glazed Salmon and I got Kung Pao Shrimp. He wasn't hip to P. F. Chang's until I told him how much I loved their Kung Pao Shrimp maybe like the first week we were talking. Ever since, we get their food like once a week.

Instead of going to Marco's house, we came back to mine, which we had been doing a lot lately. Not that I mind us coming to my house, but I did notice the change. Normally when guys start switching up their patterns it's because of a reason. I was trying not to assume or think differently about Marco, but little stuff always adds up to a big boom in the end. We're only friends, and I'm not looking for anything too serious right now, but I also don't want to be caught up in his bullshit if he's involved with another female.

"What you wanna watch?" Marco questioned as he scrolled through the options of the firestick.

"We need to catch up on *Power*. I tried not to watch it without you, but I was tempted this morning." I confessed.

"How you gon' be tempted to watch it without me and I'm the one who got you watching it. Ain't you the one who was saying you just couldn't get into it. Now look at you, hooked." He joked.

"I know right." I laughed. Once I got our drinks and utensils from the kitchen, I joined Marco in the living room on the couch so we could eat and watch TV together.

As we ate our dinner, I noticed how Marco kept looking over at me and smiling while I was eating. Normally, it doesn't make me uncomfortable when a guy watches me eats but he kept doing it.

"Why you keep eying me like that?" I questioned.

"No reason in particular. Why? Is it a problem for me to keep looking at you?"

"No, just a little weird considering we supposed to be watching *Power* and eating." I joked.

"We are watching *Power* and eating, but I enjoy the sight of you as well."

"Aww, isn't that cute. I swear you forever trying to gas me up."

"Nah baby, I ain't trying to gas you up. We can ride on E as far as I'm concerned. I just be memorized by you, I swear."

"Why is that?"

"It just be seeming too good to be true. I mean, look at you. You're beautiful, good head on your shoulder, priorities in check, mad coo, everything about you just seems so perfect. I be looking to find something wrong, but I haven't." He said as he shrugged his shoulders.

"I'm not perfect, though, and I don't want you to ever put me in the perfect category because I'll fall short. I appreciate you noticing all the qualities about me and feeling that way. I sometimes wonder the same about you but lately things been seeming a little off." I said while giving him a side-eye.

"What you mean? What's off? Talk to me baby." Marco put his fork down and focused his attention on me.

"Nothing too much. I just notice lately we haven't been by your house nor have you invited me over. It's like my house has been our default go to and that's not how things started out. It's not a problem. I just pay attention to little stuff like that."

"I respect it. I'm glad you pay attention to little stuff like that because that means you paying attention to me. You're right but it's not like I'm trying to hide anything from you. Truth be told, some things have changed with my living situation, and I just choose to spend as little time at my house as possible. Nothing that will affect you which is why I didn't say anything to you about it."

"Things changed like what, though, if that's not too much to ask." My mind got to wandering because if it wasn't a change that affected me why was he hiding it from me? What type of situation could it be to have him avoiding his nice ass home?

"It's not too much for you to ask. It's just not my place to discuss the situation. We got two extra roommates temporarily so until our house goes back to normal, I just rather keep my private life which now includes you, private." Before I could respond, he put his hand up and cut me off.

"Let me rephrase that because the way your eyebrows went up, I can tell you took it the wrong way. I'm saying, I'm not trying to keep you private or a secret cause if you ain't caught the hint by now I'm trying to make something of this between you and me. What I meant is I don't like people in my business and when I'm home I want to be comfortable and free. I don't want to watch what I say or do worried about the next person watching

or listening for some gossip. If that makes better sense." His comment about us made me blush although I tried to hide it.

"It makes sense and thanks for clarifying it. I wasn't trying to pry in your business. I just didn't want no drama to occur out of nowhere and it be a surprise to me."

"Nah baby. That's one thing you ain't got to worry about. Me and drama are two things that don't mix. I'm not bout to have you in no drama or bring no drama your way. I just wanna see you smile and make your life easier in any way I can." Little comments like such and his consistency made me want to stop holding out and give Marco some ass, but the time wasn't right.

Lord knows I'm overdue when it comes to some penetration, but I didn't want to rush it. I'm the type of chick if I'm not fucking it's not problem but the moment I start it's hard to stop. To avoid messing around with Marco and it being a waste, I chose to hold out a little longer.

We finished up our food and cuddled up on the couch watching *Power*. Being around Marco and getting to know him has been nothing but good so far. I just don't want to change things between us right now. Although I enjoy his company, every man has a dark side, and I don't know what his consists of just yet.

Neoshi

"Girl you ain't gave that man the pussy yet? What the fuck is you waiting on. Yawl been talking now for what two months. Shit, we bout to go on month three and yawl still taking it slow. I know your pussy done cussed you out by now, shit!" I fussed into the phone at Cassie.

"Shut up. HE ain't complaining so why are you?"

"How the fuck you know he ain't complaining. Of course, he ain't gon' say shit to you cause he scared that's gon' push the date for him to get some ass back even further. As many damn dates he done took you out on should be enough to give the nigga a sample at least. What the hell you waiting on?"

"My ass don't have a price tag thank you."

"OK, so what the fuck is the hold up? What yawl waiting on? You see me and Dave plays no games. We be fucking like two horny ass teenagers." I said and we both bust out into laughter.

"It's not like I'm waiting on anything in particular. I just don't wanna rush nothing. It seems like the moment you give a nigga some ass they switch up or wanna get stupid serious. It never stays the same after you have sex with a person. I ain't looking for no boyfriend, Neo. I just enjoy our friendship and his company right now." Cassie tried to justify her reasoning but it still ain't make sense to me.

"So, if you enjoy the man then give him some ass. You never know, getting some dick from him might make you realize he ain't all what you think he is. Or hell it might even change your mind and you want the nigga to be yours. You never know until you try."

"Whatever. I'm bout to go back inside the building. My lunch almost over. I'll call you when I get off."

"Enjoy the rest of you day boo."

"You too." Cassie said, and we ended our call.

Today had been slow at work. Normally, Thursdays and Fridays are busy but for some reason it's not. Working in a dentist office I have to deal with people all day long, so it feels good to not be busy but then again, it's boring. Scrolling through my news feed seeing so many cute ass couple memes about upcoming spring break I decided to text Dave. No, we ain't a couple, but shit, I could use a sponsor with dick benefits on a mini vacation.

Me: Wyd Mister?

Dave: Nothing, thinking about your slim thick ass.

Me: Here you go. Lol.

Dave: What's up? Wyd? You off today?

Me: No, we slow so I'm bored as hell.

Dave: Let me find out you only texting me cause you bored.

Me: Never. I actually was thinking about doing a spring break get away with the four of us. What you think?

Dave: Shit, I'm wit it. I know Marco gon' be with it too. Get it together and let me know the details.

Me: Will do. I'll call you when I get off work.

Dave: Bet

I immediately got on Expedia and started looking up package deals to Miami. They had some pretty decent prices and flight times. I needed to run my idea by Cassie to make sure she was on board before I got my hopes up. I hadn't been out of Ohio in so long, I was overexcited.

I screenshotted a couple of deals I liked best and sent them all to Cassie. I would verbally talk to her about them once I got off work but for now, I needed her to look through them and pick her favorites as well. Dave gave me permission to set everything up, so my guess is him and Marco just going with whatever flow me and Cassie are.

By the end of my workday, I had ordered all types of new bathing suits, sandals, and heels online for the trip we haven't even agreed on yet. Cassie wasted no time calling me. I hadn't even made it to my car from clocking out before my phone was ringing.

"What's up boo?" I greeted her when I answered the phone.

"Hey boo. What's all these damn packages you sent me about?"

"So, while I was at work bored today, I came up with the idea of a spring break trip with Dave and Marco. What you think?"

"A spring break trip don't sound bad to me. Who funding this trip? Also have you talked to them about it cause Marco hasn't mentioned nothing to me about it."

"I ran the idea passed Dave and he was all for it; he is going to talk to Marco. Of course, they goin fund it. Well, at least I know Dave ass better. I don't think Marco would expect you to pay for a trip when he doesn't even allow you to pay for your own food."

"I guess you got a point there. So, what made you pick Miami of all places. I mean, don't get me wrong. I love Miami but that's so traditional. I wanna go somewhere we never been." Cassie ass always got to be the difficult one to think of something that wasn't even mentioned.

"Traditional? Bitch please; it's spring break, everywhere on the globe is traditional shit. Where else you trying to go then if we don't do Miami."

"Hell, I don't know. I just don't wanna do Miami. I don't know. I just think we should go somewhere else. Maybe an island or something. Hell, even Vegas would be better. I just don't think you should take sand to a beach. We all single technically so being on a beach with others might be kind of awkward."

"Yeah we are all technically single but how would that be awkward?" I was confused as to what would be the difference from when we are in Columbus and out in public with them.

"I'm saying what if you see a guy eyeing you that you like. You can't talk to him; well, I mean you can, but what type of confusion would come from that?"

"Oh, I see what you're saying, but shit, that could be the case anywhere we go. I'm not against going to no island though." I said and we both busted out laughing.

"Talk to Dave and I'll talk to Marco and see what they say as far as places to go and we can go from there."

"Sounds like a plan. I already done ordered all types of shit like spring break next week or something."

"I bet you did with your eager ass but watch me start shopping soon as I talk to Marco."

"Right. Ok, this Dave calling now. Call me after you talk to Marco, so we can get this shit booked."

"Ok, I'll call you later tonight."

After ending the call between Cassie and I, I called Dave only to be sent to voicemail. Instead of sending a text through, I called again just to make sure the nigga really did red button me. Once again, my call was sent to voicemail. Dave ain't my nigga, but I can't stand to be ignored, and that was enough for me to shoot him an ignorant text.

Dave is coo and all but one thing I won't do is let a nigga play me ever again. I'm single, so there are always options available. I just don't wanna be fucking around with multiple niggas at once. Don't get it twisted, though, because I can straight add another nigga to my roster no problem. Keeping my options open is my first level of defense when it comes to getting too close to these niggas.

Dave

Ever since the day Neoshi mentioned something about Spring Break it seems like Nyia been on her A game. Like she ain't been trying to argue or fight with a nigga to save her life. She still fails to mention or talk about her move-out date and we going on almost month two of her staying with us. The only good that has come of her staying with us is me being with my son more. Other than that, it's been miserable.

I can say I stuck to my grounds when I said I wouldn't fuck her though. Just last night, she crept up in my room in the middle of the night with just her robe on. Being woke out your sleep to somebody trying to suck your dick normally is a nigga's dream come true. Nah, not me. I woke up like a straight bitch. Imagine a nigga damn near six feet tall waking up kicking and screaming for a bitch to leave him alone. I felt violated like a muthafucka.

Bad enough I been in the house for the past couple of days cause my son sick. Nyia been working and I refuse for her excuse to be she can't afford her new place so she needs to run them checks up while she can. I been missing Neoshi little ass over these two days, though, I can't lie. She mad at a nigga right now but once I explain I been with my son, hopefully, she'll understand. I noticed she been real short with me lately, and that's the first sign of a bitch feeling some type of way.

If it was up to me, I would have Neoshi come over to the crib since I'm stuck in the house with my son but I know that shit wouldn't fly with Nyia living here. I mean, eventually, if Neoshi stick around and stop with all this remaining friends bullshit, she gon' have to be around my son. Now just ain't the time and my crib ain't the place. Nyia would swear up and down she my bitch then and it would really be some messy shit in the atmosphere. Some shit I ain't even trying to deal with.

Marco ass tired of adjusting his life around my inconvenience of a baby mom. Last night he even asked Nyia how shit was going with her job and new place in casual conversation. If she ain't take that as a hint I don't know what else she will.

"I'm bout to run to the liquor store. You want me to grab you a bottle?" Marco announced as he headed towards the door.

"Hell yeah! It's gon' be a long ass day with no liquor in this bitch if not." I replied as I sprang to my feet and headed upstairs to grab some money.

"Grab me two Liters of Hennessy VSOP." I said and I handed Marco my money.

"Damn nigga how much you plan on drinking today?" He joked.

"I ain't bout to drink all that shit today foo. I just might as well grab two now instead of one now and one tomorrow. If this little nigga doesn't break this fever I'mma be in this bitch another few days going crazy." I don't know what type of virus my son had, but I was ready for it to break and he go back to daycare. I ain't for the stay-at-home dad roll. Certain moves I just ain't cut out for and this is one. I get credit where credit is due, but I don't even want this type of credit. A nigga patience ain't built for it.

DJ was dozing off on the couch, so I decided to give Neoshi another call while I had some quiet time. When she answered the phone, I damn near jumped out my skin like a straight bitch. I honestly wasn't expecting her to pick up.

"Damn, what's up with my boo? Why I ain't heard from you? You avoiding a nigga or what? Let me know something."

"Ain't nobody ignoring your ass, chill." Neoshi responding nonchalantly.

"Yeah ok. You say that shit but my unanswered calls and texts left on read say something different. What's up with up? You ain't feeling me no more? Damn my heart is crushed. I ain't think you was gon' quit me this soon."

"Heartbroken? You funny Dave. Ain't nobody hurt you boy. Ain't nothing up though. Same shit just a different day. Working, you know my routine."

"You right I do, and I was part of it but lately I'm feeling played."

"Whatever. What you doing?"

"Nothing, waiting on Marco to get back from the liquor store. Just laid my son down for a nap."

"It's kind of early for the liquor store ain't it?" I knew she was gon' talk shit about me drinking this early in the day; she always does.

"Hell nah, it's never too early when you dealing with a sick baby crying all damn morning. This is the what? Third day in a row? That shit takes a toll on your mental."

"It can't be that bad. Are you staying on top of his fluids and medicine?"

"Yeah but that shit only seems to calm the storm for a quick second then he back on a roll. It don't help the nigga don't know how to talk. Shit all I understand is dad, juice and ouch. How the fuck I'm supposed to work through that?"

"I don't know but it sounds like you better figure it out and quick." Neoshi even laughed at her last comment.

"I am; that's why I'm day drinking."

"You just needed an excuse to day drink, shut up."

"Ok, you might have a point but we not gon' dwell on that. You on your lunch still?" I decided to stop beating around the bush.

"Nope, I'm off. I only worked a half of day. I had some shit to take care of."

"Let me find out."

"Let you find out what?" She questioned.

"Let me find out you fucking around with a new nigga that got you taking off work early and shit. You never did that for me." I complained trying to pull something out of her about her messing around.

"Please, ain't no dick got me calling out. I could neva."

"Oh, well come see me real quick." I said looking at the time seeing that I had a good three hours before Nyia would be off of work.

"You got your son Dave." I knew she was gon' come back with that bullshit excuse.

"Ok and I just told you he sleep. You ain't gotta stay around I just wanna see your face and squeeze that booty fa real."

"I bet you do. I'll stop by while I'm on this side of town, but I can't stay too long. I gotta meet Cassie in thirty mins."

"That's coo. I ain't trying to fuck. I just wanna see you and touch you fa real. I mean, getting this big muthafucka wet would be nice but I ain't that bold. Just my luck, this nigga wake up mid-stroke and fuck my whole shit up."

"Man bye. I'll see you in a minute." Neoshi said and ended the call before I could even respond.

A good five minutes passed, and I saw her car pull into the driveway from the camera system. Hurrying to the door I decided to greet her at the door, but my phone rang before I could reach the door.

"I'm opening the door now." I said soon as I answered.

"Just run out real quick. Cassie ass already waiting on me so I gotta leave sooner than I expected."

I hung up the phone and slid my Nike slides on to head outside to see her. Just as I got to the driver side of the car, I couldn't help but lick my lips when I laid eyes on her up close. Neoshi got out the car and looked me up and down as if she was inspecting me before giving me a hug. When she reached up to wrap her arms around my neck and embrace me, I took advantage and locked her in my arms. Squeezing not only her waist with my arms, I make sure to get a good two handfuls of them cheeks.

She gave me a peck on the cheek and got back into her car, promising to call me when she finished up with Cassie. Just as Neoshi pulled off and was turning off the street, I be damn if Nyia wasn't pulling up from the opposite direction. I damn near ran in the house but instead I played it coo. I had to remind myself whose house it was and my relationship status.

Nyia

As bad as I wanted to believe my eyes were playing tricks on me, I knew they weren't. I saw a car pull out the driveway of the house when I turned on the street and Dave standing outside in his basketball shorts, tank top and Nike slides. The car that pulled out was a red newer Honda, so I knew it wasn't Marco.

No one ever comes to the house, so I knew for sure Dave didn't have any of his niggas coming by. Considering that Marco didn't rock with half of the dudes they used to hang around, Dave keeps his distance too from them. Ross don't drive no Honda and neither does his baby mom. The only thing that came to mind was it had to be a bitch.

I know this nigga ain't got the balls to have another bitch around my son and in the house I'm laying my head at every night. Just blatantly disrespectful. I thought to myself.

The moment I walked in the house Dave started questioning what I was doing off work so early. That was the first clue that he was up to no good. I simply rolled my eyes at him and headed to the basement so I could shower and get out of my work clothes before going to give my baby some loving while he was asleep peacefully on the couch near where Dave sat.

As I let the hot beads of water drip down my skin, I couldn't help but let a few tears escape my eyes. The longer I stood there, the more my thoughts taunted me. It hurt to know that no matter how hard I tried Dave resisted my love and our connection even more. It was no secret he no longer wanted to be with me or be a family; it just hurt accepting it. I can't see myself letting a new bitch come into the picture and get the new and improved Dave.

All those years I invested into him would all be a waste. I was here when he was a nickel and dime ass hustler using my car to make his runs. Now that he is financially established and owns businesses, I refuse to sit back and watch another bitch reap the benefits of my hard work. Whether they are big businesses or not it the point that he has his own income and is his own boss.

My shower was much longer than I thought. When I finished getting dressed, I looked at the time on my phone and noticed that forty-five minutes had passed since I first walked into the house. I headed upstairs to take something out to eat for dinner for DJ and me. Even though I had been cooking meals for the entire house, I for sure wasn't tonight. Dave and Marco would have to fend for themselves. It's not like they appreciate it no way. Well, I take that back. I actually think Marco appreciates my work around the house more than Dave does, and that's a fucking problem.

"When is the last time he had some medicine? He feels hot Dave!" I said as I rubbed my cheek against DJ's.

"Like an hour ago. He just had fell asleep before you got here." Dave replied with his attention fixed on his phone.

"Oh, ok maybe he just feels hot cause he on the damn leather couch." I replied and picked DJ up so I could take him upstairs to Dave's bed to sleep.

Once DJ was secured in the middle of Dave's King size bed, I headed downstairs to start prepping the items I took out for dinner. Tonight, would be something quick and easy. Tuna Casserole is my favorite quick, easy meal to cook and eat. I also know, not only does Dave hate the smell of tuna, but he won't eat it; I have an excuse now for only making a personal pan big enough for me and my baby. DJ normally has a big appetite for a year old but him being sick I knew he wouldn't eat much.

"Man, of all the damn things to cook when you get off early, you pick fucking tuna. Really? Tuna? Who the fuck just wants to eat tuna and noodles with cheese sprinkled on top? That shit shouldn't even be considered a meal." Dave fussed the moment he walked in the kitchen and saw what I was preparing.

"You ain't gotta eat what I cook so why are you complaining. That's all you ever do anymore, is complain. Do you ever stop and think of the shit you say before you say it? Sometimes your smart comments are not necessary." I was trying not to go the fuck off on Dave, but he was pushing my buttons for no reason.

"Actually, no I don't think about what I'm going say before I say it. What the fuck purpose does that serve. I'm not bout to strategize how to express what the fuck I feel. I do people a good service by adding my two cents. You need to actually listen so time. You ain't gon' ever get a fucking husband cooking shit like Tuna Casserole every got damn night. Don't nobody wanna eat the chicken of the sea, da fuck!"

"Dave, go the fuck on somewhere. I ain't bout to argue with you about what I'm cooking me and my son for dinner."

"Our son don't want that shit either. But if it makes you feel good inside whip that shit up then girl."

"There you go being funny. Go on somewhere Dave."

"I sure am. Right to my living room to enjoy Netflix and wait for Marco to return with my damn drank!" Dave said and walked out the kitchen in the direction of the living room.

Once I eat, I'm going to the basement and just staying to myself for the rest of the night. It's best that Dave and I stay out of each other's paths until I calm down. I don't wanna spazz out on him and say something I'm going to regret.

Casanae

Marco been working his ass off to get my undivided attention, and I must say it's working. I'm still on edge a little bit because I still don't know the full situation of what is going on with his living situation. I'm almost ready to do a pop up on him, but I feel like that would me doing too much. Like, I still ain't gave him no ass yet, so how do I have the right to question him?

Although he hasn't pressured me, I know he's wondering when is that time going to be over with. We going on three months of knowing and talking to each other. I feel like I've known Marco much longer than three months just because we vibe so well together. My level of comfortability with him is unreal.

When I spoke with Marco about the spring break trip, he told me he was already thinking about doing something similar so of course he was on board. He agreed with me that Vegas or out of the country would be better than Miami. When I told him that Neoshi and I had been online shopping he told me not to buy anything else. I pretended as if I was going to comply with his statement, but it was too late. I honestly had already purchased my entire wardrobe for our mini vacation. The only thing I hadn't purchased yet were my travel size hygiene products.

Lounging around on the couch doing absolutely nothing besides snacking and binge-watching *Ozark*, I was interrupted by my phone ringing.

"Hey Mr.!" I greeted Marco.

"What's up Beautiful?"

"Nothing much. What's up with you?"

"Wanting to see your face." Marco confessed.

"Why wouldn't you facetime me then?" I questioned. With technology the level it is that sounded pretty cheesy to me.

"That ain't good enough. Open the door." I immediately looked around my front room and then hopped up to run to my bedroom and put some shorts on. Considering I was home alone and lounging around, I was only dressed in an oversized tee shirt and my panties. No socks, no bra, and no bottoms.

"What's taking you so long to open the door?" Marco questioned as I tried to hurry back down to open the door for him.

"I had to run and throw something on. I wasn't expecting any company." I said as I was opening the door. When we made eye contact neither of us could help but to smile as we ended our call.

Marco walked into my house and immediately wrapped his arms around my waist. He pulled me in for a hug while planting two soft kisses on my forehead. I don't know why but when he does that, it makes me feel like the prettiest girl in the world.

"You should've warned me. I'm laying in here looking a mess, chilling. I did not expect to see anyone this early." I complained as I ran my fingers through my hair.

"Baby you straight. You look just fine to me. You don't ever have to worry about getting all dolled up and shit to see me. I'm pleased to see you in any form. True beauty shows at all hours." Of course, here came the blushing.

"Man, you just don't know what you do to a nigga when you start blushing. Making me feel all soft and shit." Marco complained in a joking way.

"I can't help it; imagine how you make me feel. Considering the fact that I'm dark skinned it shouldn't be this easy for you to see me getting all flushed and shit. It's embarrassing. Making me feel all bashful."

"Aww baby, don't be bashful." Marco said before giving me another forehead kiss before we headed over to the couch.

"What we bout to watch?" Marco questioned as he leaned forward and started removing his shoes.

"Umm, I was watching *Ozark*. You wanna watch this or something else?"

"Nah *Ozark* is coo. I actually started watching it a couple of nights ago, but I fell asleep and only finished two episodes of season one."

"Perfect, cause I'm only on episode three of season one. How long you gon' be here? I was about to order me a pizza and some wings. I don't plan on leaving this couch today."

"I'm staying here as long as you allow. I don't have no plans today. Well, none other than being up under you. I'm coo with pizza and wings. Where we getting it from?"

"I was thinking Marco's. I haven't had none of their pizza in a while."

"You want me to order it online or you got it?" He questioned as he pulled his phone from his pocket and started typing in the Safari search bar. I loved the initiative that Marco always takes no matter how big or small the situation.

"It doesn't matter. Make sure you get extra cheese."

"So large extra cheese pep, with jalapenos? What kind of wings you want? Boneless or bone-in and what flavor?"

"I'm thinking barbeque wings and bone-in."

"You want me to go pick it up cause delivery says an hour and pickup only fifteen minutes. By the time I get there the food will be ready."

"Pick up please. I'll ride with you if you want me to. I said as I stood from the couch preparing myself to go get dressed really quick.

"Nah, you stay here. You didn't plan on leaving the couch so have a seat. I'll be right back. You want anything else while I'm out?"

"No thank you." I said and took my seat back on the couch where I was originally sitting.

Marco placed his shoes back on his feet and headed out the door. If I knew for sure Marco would never switch up or change on me, I wouldn't have a problem getting used to him being around for the long ride.

While Marco was out grabbing the food, I decided to call Neo to see how her Thursday was going. I knew she would be on her lunch break, so I wouldn't be interrupting her workflow.

As expected, she was talking to Dave, so she rushed off the phone. It's cute, funny and aggy all at the same time. Neo swears up and down she don't want a relationship but other than a title her and Dave are already in a relationship. They both territorial and only sleeping with each other so why not just make it official?

Since talking to Neo didn't pass the time until Marco got back, Toon Blast it was. This damn game occupies every break when I'm at work and sometimes when I'm at home. It's crazy how addicting these damn phone games are.

Just as I expected, time flew by a lot faster with my attention fixed on my phone. Before I could even run out of all my lives, Marco was walking in the house with food in hand. He even stopped by the corner store and grabbed me a lemonade Everfresh although I told him I didn't want anything else. Marco pays close attention to the things I like and my habits. Everfresh is my drug of choice. I have to have at least two a day or I'm craving them like a junky.

"Thanks babe." I said as I kissed him on the cheek to show my gratitude.

"It's no problem beautiful." He replied.

Marco headed to the living room as I prepared our plates. Once our plates were made, I took them to the living room and headed back for our drinks and napkins. Although it was only takeout pizza, it's still a woman's place to make the man's plate and serve him.

As we ate our food and watched *Ozark* together, we discussed our up and coming spring break trip. After comparing and further research, we decided on going to Vegas instead of out the country. The main reason we decided on staying withing the US was because Marco nor Dave had passports and the only way to get them within the next two weeks would be to expedite and in my opinion that was a waste of money. We could always travel out the country at a later date. Besides, none of us had ever been to Vegas.

Marco

I been ready to give Casanae the business, but I could tell she was playing the waiting game. I don't know her aim for the wait but I'm willing to be patient and see what the outcome will be. Just my luck once we cross that line she gon' either be crazy as fuck or her attitude gon' change. I'm hoping it doesn't for my sake but that seems to be how things tend to work out.

At the age of twenty-seven years old, I feel like I'm ready to settle down and start having babies. Something about Casanae makes me feel like she's the one. Even on the days where she's a little bitchy and in them moods females go through, I still wouldn't mind being with her for the long haul. I'm hoping our trip to Vegas seals the deal for our little thing we got going.

"Is there something still going on at your house? Is that why we been kicking at my house a hell of a lot more lately?" Casanae questioned entered the freeway in the direction of her house.

"Look Casanae, I been nothing but honest with you since the first time I spoke to you. I don't want you to think it's some sneaky shit going on, on my behalf. Then again it's honestly not my place to go in details about the situation either."

"I'm not doubting that you've ever lied to me, but I also feel like you hiding some of the truth. Although it may not be your place to tell me it involves you, so I don't understand how it doesn't." Dave is my brah but I'm beyond tired of tip toeing around the living situation with Nyia.

"You're right. And if it takes for me to show you better than avoid telling you then that's what I'll do. I don't want you to start feeling any type of way about me when it's not deserved." I said as I took the next exit to reroute in the direction of my crib.

Unsure on how the situation was about to play out I just rode the remainder of the way in silence. I knew Dave wouldn't give a fuck as far as Nyia was concerned but Neoshi's thoughts and feeling on this situation might be the part he ain't too pleased about. As a man he's gon' have to respect where I'm coming from and see my reasoning behind it.

The moment we pulled into my driveway, I let out a deep sigh. I can't say if it was from frustration, nervousness, or relief. Casanae looked over at me then turned to look in the direction of Nyia's car then back at me. My guess is since she knew what type of car Dave drove, she already had some type of idea about what was going on inside.

"You ready?" I questioned Casanae.

"When you are." She replied and I exited the car. As I walked around the car to open her door, I could see the look of seriousness on her face.

"Why you looking like that?" I questioned with a snicker to lighten the mood some.

"Looking like what?" She giggled back and seemed to ease up some.

I could hear Nyia and Dave arguing loud and clear before the keys were turned in the locks. I walked in first and allowed Casanae to follow instead of letting her lead as normal. I didn't know what type of argument the two of them were having, and I didn't want Nyia to try no shit with Casanae if she saw her walk in before me.

"Brah, I'm not trying to hear that shit. You was been supposed to had your shit up outta here. You draggin your ass on moving cause you feel like my mind going change about you, us and this fairytale you got made up in your head but I'm not." Dave yelled from upstairs in whatever direction Nyia was.

"Fairytale, oh that's what you call this? That's what you think trying to work things out with you for the sake of our son is? A fairytale. Huh? You gotta be fucking kidding me. More like a got damn nightmare. I've never met a more unappreciative ass nigga in my life." Nyia yell from the kitchen still not realizing that me and Casanae had walked into the house.

"If it's so much of a got damn nightmare, wake the fuck up and move out. What's stopping you cause it damn sure ain't me. That would be a fucking fairytale."

"Yeah, ok bitch!" Nyia yelled. I knew that was going to blow a fuse with Dave. One thing you don't do is call a man no bitch.

"Bitch?" I heard Dave yell and his footsteps coming down the stairs quick as fuck. The moment he looked over and saw me and Casanae he stopped in his tracks.

"What's up Marco? What's up Cassie?" Dave greeted us both.

"Hey!" Casanae spoke back as I gave him a head nod.

"This unstable ass creature is going to make me catch a fucking case. I'm bout to get outta here before I do some shit I'mma regret." Dave said as he grabbed his keys off the coffee table. Had we not been standing in the middle of the living room he probably would've went in that kitchen and slap the dog piss out of Nyia.

"Bet. I'm bout to head right back out. Had I known all this was going on I would've held off coming back to the crib." I confessed. I wanted Casanae to know I wasn't hiding anything from her, but I also didn't want her all in Dave business. It was too late for that now, she had witnessed it all.

"Where the fuck are you go…" Nyia was caught by surprise to see a woman standing in the middle of our living room. She couldn't even finish her sentence.

"See, look at your stupid ass, looking like a got damn foo. Just can't leave shit alone. When you heard me stop that's when you should've shut the fuck up. But no, that's your problem. You don't know how to shut the fuck up."

"You know what Dave, Fuck you!" Nyia said and turned to walk towards the basement.

"See what I mean; she just can't shut the fuck up! Brah, I'mma hit you up once I ease my nerves. I gotta calm down some." Dave said as he walked out the front door and we followed behind him.

I can't imagine what I would do if I was in his shoes. Certain levels of stress I can't handle. It's only so much I can take before I crash out and take things to a level I'll end up regretting.

We were halfway to Casanae's place and she still hadn't said a word. I don't know if it was because she was in shock from what happened at my crib. She doesn't take me for a drama or confrontational type so that could be it. Or it could be because she doesn't know what to say. Either way we would for sure have a detailed conversation tonight.

Neoshi

It had been a week almost of me keeping it coo and pretending that shit was sweet between Dave and I. When Cassie told me about the altercation at Dave's house, I almost didn't want to believe her, but I know my girl wasn't lying. Cassie and I been best friends since we were in middle school. Her loyalty to me wouldn't let her keep something like that from me.

A part of me was pissed the fuck off that his baby mom had been staying there. It all made sense now why he wasn't available as much as he was when we first started fucking around. Then the other side of me was happy to know that they weren't in a good place with each other. I think the fact that I didn't know whether or not they'd always been this way, or if it was only for the moment that had me on edge. As far as I'm concerned, she could've been living there all along and they could just be at odds.

Years of being fucked over by a nigga who claimed to love me only makes me think the worse of all niggas, especially a nigga I'm just fucking on with no commitment. It's safe to say I don't trust Dave. I mean, over the course of four months I've gotten to know him well, but you never fully know a person that quick.

If it wasn't for this trip we preplanned I more than likely would have ignored Dave until I was good and ready. It's so bad I didn't even want him to pick me up so we could all ride to the airport together. I had Cassie pick me up and we took an Uber to the airport. Although Marco bout had a fit on Cassie for us taking an Uber, she calmed him down enough to stop tripping.

I pretended to be so tired and taking a nap until we needed to board the plane just to avoid conversation with Dave until I got some sort of alcohol in my system. I wanted to come to the airport drunk, but Cassie had to remind me if I was over a certain level, they wouldn't allow me to fly. The moment we get in the air and the flight attendants come around for orders I'm running his got damn tab up on whatever drink they have that's dark.

Three hours and countless drinks later we had finally landed in Vegas. I couldn't wait to step off that airplane. Walking through the airport I was surprised to see people in areas smoking and slots every were. I mean I know Vegas is known for gambling but literally everywhere I looked there was a slot machine.

There was a chauffeur awaiting our arrival holding a sign in the air with mine and Cassie's name right by baggage claim. Marco didn't pack any luggage so all he had was Cassie's one suitcase. Dave, on the other hand, look like he was struggling carrying the both of our bags. Not only was he pulling both of our rolling suitcases, but he was carrying both of our duffle bags. Dave packed just as much as I did. Thank goodness for Southwest two free bag incentive or we would've spent a good two hundred plus on our luggage alone one way.

I was enjoying sightseeing as we rode to the hotel. Seeing mountains and dessert areas in pictures compared to in person is so different. Pictures do no justice for how beautiful everything is in Nevada. There were dispensary advertisements everywhere. Normally I'm not a smoker but I know for sure I'm going to sample some form of weed while I'm down here. I mean it's legal why not?

Hard Rock Hotel and Casino would be our homes for the next week. Marco and Cassie have a separate suite from Dave and I of course. Depending on how things go between Dave and I, I might fuck around and get my own suite.

"What's wrong with my boo. You feeling alright or you jet-lagged?" Dave questioned as the door to our room closed behind him.

"No, I'm not jet lagged. I'm ready to hit the strip. I'm coo." I lied and tried to play it as smooth as I could.

"You just don't seem like yourself, but if you say you're ok I'm going to take your word for it."

"Nah I'm coo, don't worry."

"Ight, so we hitting the strip now or we changing first?" Dave questioned.

"Yeah, I wanna wash off and change first then we out." I said in reply eagerly still feeling somewhat of a buzz from all the drinks I had on the plane.

"I hope you don't got no skimpy ass shorts to change into. Better have something to cover up them cheeks I know that much." Dave fussed as I grabbed my duffle bag and headed into the bathroom.

"Hush, it's hot as fuck out here. I hope you don't think I'm going to be covered up like it's against my religion or something just to show some skin. My clothes are just fine." I knew better than to pack a bunch of skimpy shit on a vacation I was going on with a nigga I'm fucking. That would be grounds to argue our entire trip. I knew how to keep it cute and still show skin without looking like I was giving a free peep show.

The first place we stopped once we were dressed was Medmen dispensary. Being directly across from our hotel it was in walking distance. When we walked inside, they asked for our ID, registered us an account and then allowed us to browse freely. Dave wasn't a smoker, but little did he know we would both be trying something new while we were here.

Needless to say, Dave bought a bunch of shit. I had no clue how we would get back to Ohio on a plane but that was for him to figure out. I grabbed a variety box of pre rolled joints to try out. There was a joint for every strand of weed that exist and a few joints that were mixtures of different strands. Each day I planned to try a different one. Me not being a smoker I'm sure the little variety box will not be completed before we leave here.

Right next door to the dispensary was a liquor store. I knew that was right where Dave wanted to be so without question, I headed there next. Their liquor seemed to be much cheaper than ours back home, which made no sense to me but I'm all for the deal. When Dave walked from the back of the liquor store with two arms full of liquor, I couldn't help but laugh.

"Why you got all them bottles?" I laughed as I questioned him.

"Shit it's stupid cheap. Why not. We going be here for a week, somebody gon' drink it." Dave said in his defense.

"You do understand we drink for free in the Casino's right?" It made no sense to me for him to buy that much liquor when we could drink for free.

"I ain't know that but I'm sure that shit is bottom shelf and watered down. I'll just keep my shit refilled of my own product. Ain't nobody bout to slip me not mickey, roofie or nothing else while I'm down here." I just shook my head and started laughing. The shit that comes out of Dave's mouth is ridiculous.

We headed back to our room to drop off the goodies we had just purchased. The ninety-degree weather in mid-April was different than what we were used to back home in Ohio. I immediately changed my shirt to a thin tank top I had to match the stone washed bermuda shorts.

"Got damn back was baking wasn't it?" Dave joked referring to the black tee shirt I had on originally.

"Hell yeah." I joked back.

Once changed, we headed back out. Instead of taking an Uber to the strip we decided to walk and sight see along the way. Once we reached the stirp there were so many attractions and stores, I felt like a kid in the middle of the candy store. All type of designer stores, restaurants, other casinos, and much more.

"You gon' light one of your little joints up or you gon' wait until later?" Dave questioned as we crossed the street so I could explore what the Louis Vuitton store had to offer.

"I'm going to light it, but I'm going to wait until after I see what's inside this store."

"You might be able to light it up in there. I mean, it is legal."

"Yeah right. It ain't that sweet down here."

"You right. I'm just bullshitting." Dave laughed off his last statement.

Dave

Coming to Vegas wasn't my original choice of vacation destinations, but it was damn sure worth it. I imagined being on a beach some got damn where not in the damn dessert. As hot as it is here, I feel like we walking through sand towards our destination and the sun beaming down on us. The fact that we could freely smoke weed and drink cheap ass liquor was for sure a good replacement for a beach. I'm not a weed smoker, but I bet I get high while I'm here just for the hell of it.

This break away from Nyia and my son was needed though. Not so much my son, but his momma. I had to get the hell away from her before I fucked around and choked her out the game. The longer she's at my crib, the more I regret ever saying she could stay. I'll never say I regret my son, but the choice of his mother is for damn sure at the top of my list.

Nyia asked all types of questions about where we were going, who was going with us, how long we would be gone, and the purpose of us going. I didn't feel like any of it was her business to be concerned with, so I dismissed her ass every time she questioned me about this trip. I'm sure she assumed we were, either going to meet up with some bitches, or be with some bitches, and she was damn right. It's not that I care if she knows I'm here with another woman, but I wasn't going to piss her off before I left town. The last thing I needed was to come home to any of my shit being fucked up. Nyia is that type of bitter bitch.

She will for sure take out her frustration on anything in her sight. Been down that path one too many times in the past.

I had really been contemplating putting Nyia out after this vacation anyway, but I'm on the fence about it just on the strength I don't want her to put my son in the middle. Depending on how she acts while I'm on this trip, it will determine if I put her out soon as I get back or not.

I'm tired of hiding the situation from Neoshi. I think the change in routine is starting to cause Neoshi to act differently and assume shit. I planned to explain it to her after Cassie witnessed Nyia and me arguing, but she never questioned me about it, so I never brought it up either. Closed mouths don't get fed so if she don't ask I for damn sure won't tell.

We were only on day one of our vacation, and I was already realizing I wasn't going to make it in Vegas. The time change of three hours fucked me up. We been ripping and running around since the moment we landed, not even seeing a portion of the things we had planned. When we got back to the hotel, it was one in the morning, and it was still constant traffic and activity like it was one in the afternoon. My body could tell it was really four in the morning and a nigga was tired as fuck. I don't know if it was the jetlag, heat, liquor or a combination of the three.

"You still high?" I questioned Neoshi.

"I think so. I'm relaxed as hell, I know that much." Neoshi said before she got up from the couch and walked over to the bed to lay down.

"I knew your ass was gon' be high all damn day. You ain't no smoker and you kept lighting that little joint up smoking like you was a real smoker or something." I laughed at her ass.

The moment Neoshi laid in bed next to me my dick rocked up. I slowly rolled in her direction and wrapped my arms around her waist. She resisted, unlike normal, so I thrust my hips forward pressing my dick against her ass. She only had on her bra and panties, which is what she normally sleeps in. I, on the other hand, had on my briefs and that's it.

"Dave really? You ain't tired?" Neoshi questioned.

"Hell, yeah I'm tired, but not too tired for some pussy." I replied in the most serious manner. "Roll over bae." I whispered in her ear from behind and she complied.

Lifting my lower half off the bed, I used my free hand to remove my briefs. As I removed my briefs, Neoshi removed her panties and bra as well. Rolling back over, I slide my dick inside of her slowly. The warm, wet feeling of her insides had a nigga's toes curling. It had only been about four or five days since we last fucked but it felt like forever.

Neoshi was trying to hold in her moans, but I could hear her soft whimpers with each stroke. Hearing her soft moans only made me get more aggressive. Pounding in and out of her at a fast rate, I lost my rhythm and had to switch it up. Had a nigga feeling like pink meat.

"Hop on top real quick!" I commanded.

Neoshi slowly winded her hips in a circular motion as she slid down my dick. How she was able to do the things she did with my dick I had no clue, but I enjoyed it very much so.

"Got damn, Neoshi, what the fuck man!" I grunted.

Me talking to her only made her start going even harder on top of me. The sounds of her juices and her moans had me ready to call out her name. Her ass slapped my thighs as she slammed down on top of me creating its own rhythms.

"FUCK!" I yelled out in pleasure. "Slow down, you trying to make me nut." I gripped her hips to try to control her pace and hold off my nut. I felt her cumming, and it only made the sensation even stronger.

"SLOW your ass the fuck down. I ain't ready to nut!" She only sped up and started moaning even louder. "Oh, it's too much for you bae?" She questioned seductively.

"Stop …Shit… Stop playing." Between grunts and moans, I tried to tell her again.

"Dave you want me?" Neoshi moaned.

"Fuck yeah, I want you!" I honestly replied. I really wanted Neoshi for more than just sex. I wanted her to be mine but I knew that wasn't what she wanted.

"This dick belong to me?"

"Yeah, this your dick baby!" Another truth.

I hadn't fucked with any other females since I started fucking Neoshi, little did she know. The more she talked to me, the slower she winded her hips. I could feel my nut at the tip of my dick ready to be released. Normally, we use protection but tonight I was about to shoot her club up for sure.

"Then don't ever disrespect me with another bitch AGAIN!" Neoshi said through gritted teeth as she tightened her pussy muscles and got up from on top of me.

"Neoshi, stop fucking playing man." I said as my dick pulsated.

She rushed to put some shorts and a shirt on and left the room without responding. Even with me calling out after her she never turned back to even look at me.

Jumping out the bed, I rushed to the door to follow after her. Looking to my left then right down the hallway to see which direction she ran off into, I saw her damn near running towards the elevators. So, I ran after her ass. Dick slanging and all, I ain't give a fuck. I needed to finish my nut before I caught blue balls in Vegas.

"OH MY GOD!" I heard an unknown voice yell from behind me. Turning around to see what the hell she was in shock about, I realized it was me. The older, White lady got an eye full of my "big, black cock" as they would call it.

The look on her face was priceless. Seeing the shock on her face made me turn around and head back to my room, only to realize that I ran out the room so quick I left the key inside.

"FUCK!" I yelled as I wiggled the handle to my hotel room as if it was going to magically open for me.

"Excuse me maa'm." I said trying to get the ladies' attention before she was out of sight. The moment she turned to face me I used my two hands to cover my dick, looking like a fucking kid.

"Can you PLEASE call front desk and let them know we have an emergency. I'll pay you or whatever. I just need to get in my room." I said out of desperation.

"Um... Sure, why not." She said as she headed back to the room in which she came from. I was hoping like hell there wasn't no man in the room. The last thing I needed was some old ass hillbilly seeing me ass naked.

Casanae

"You scared beautiful?" Marco questioned me, and I picked my cuticles as we waited for the host to call our name.

"A little. You ain't scared?" I questioned him in return.

"Nah, I ain't scared. I don't want you scared either." Marco said as he wrapped his arm around my shoulder for comfort.

We were sitting on the bench waiting our turn at Vegas Indoor Skydiving. Although we would be indoor and have a trampoline-like net beneath us, it didn't help the fact that I was scared of heights. It looks fun but the way my stomach drops when we drive down a hill too fast, I could only imagine how my insides are about to turn when it's our turn.

After paying, we were required to put on a big jumpsuit... the kind skydivers wear. The shoes they required us to wear were weird looking tennis shoes. I don't know why we were required to change our shoes if we had on tennis shoes, but I guess the soles of the shoes were different. The protective glasses and helmet I felt were a bit extreme. Then again it may not be because the video we were required to watch prior to our participation stated that if rules weren't followed, death was a possible consequence. I don't know if they say that just to scare you into following directions or not, but I wasn't about to take any chances.

"You guys ready to see what it feels like to fly?" The instructor asked and Marco looked at me for my confirmation. I nodded my head and stood to my feet.

"It's ok baby. You'll be straight. Ain't nothing gon' happen to you." Marco tried his best to reassure me before kissing me on the forehead. I took a deep breath and decided it was time to face one of my fears.

We were inside of the skydiving area all of twenty minutes. It took us longer to pay, watch videos, and get dressed than it did for us to actually participate. I did get the same feeling in my stomach as I would on a roller coaster, but it wasn't consistent. It wasn't half as bad as I thought it would be. The strong winds that blew us around the area where more harm that the skydiving portion.

Marco went first when we were inside, and he followed the rules and was floating as if he was an expert. I, on the other hand, thought I was following the instructions given to me but obviously I wasn't. No matter how hard I tried I wouldn't go past a certain altitude. When it was over we were able to look over the pictures that were taken of us while inside.

The looks on the both of our faces were priceless. We laughed so hard at the facial expressions caught on camera. Marco couldn't decide which photos he wanted to have printed off, so he decided to purchase the video instead, which captured everything from start to finish.

"You wanna grab something to eat now or you wanna wait until after we go to the Wax Museum?"

"I'm hungry now. We can go there after we eat." I said as I rubbed my hands in a circular motion over my stomach.

"I was hoping you said that cause a nigga is starved. What you gotta taste for? Something quick or a full-course meal?"

"Whichever you prefer is fine by me."

"Coo, let's go to the Ramsay Place we walked passed earlier." I started laughing immediately.

"You mean Gordon Ramsay Hell's Kitchen?" I said while still laughing.

"Yeah, that's it. You knew what I meant."

"I didn't know actually until you said his last name then it clicked."

Instead of us walking to the restaurant, Marco requested an Uber for us to get to the restaurant. When we arrived, the crowd was super thick. I thought about changing my mind and grabbing something quick to eat instead. Just as I was about to say something to Marco, he walked over and spoke to someone. Next thing I knew they were calling our names for us to head to out table. I don't know what he said or offered, but it for sure enabled us to skip the wait.

The restaurant was very upscale, and I was thankful that we were dressed pretty casual or we for sure wouldn't have fit in.

Now the menu, on the other hand, was something else. I was pissed looking at the prices of the food. I'm not a cheap type of chick, but that shit was ridiculous. The meal I ordered was seventy damn dollars for a lunch special. Beef Wellington ain't never cost so much in my entire life. Marco didn't have a problem with it. The fact that his meal was fifty dollars and he added on twelve grams of caviar for forty-five dollars was beyond me. Ain't no way in hell I'm eating caviar let alone paying for it by grams like it's a drug or something.

Once we were done eating, I no longer wanted to go to the Wax Museum. I just wanted to head back to the room and take a nap. When we got back to the hotel, I decided to shower and lay down for a hot second. Marco showered after me and decided to go to the casino in the lobby of our hotel until I was ready to head back out.

Waking up from my nap, I was surprised when I looked over at the clock on the nightstand and read seven o'clock. I couldn't believe that I had slept for that many hours. Had I not had a sex dream about Marco I probably wouldn't have woken up when I did. I looked at my phone, and seeing missed called and texts from Neoshi, I knew she was probably trying to link up. We hadn't seen each other since we got to this hotel. I also had a text from Marco telling me to call him when I woke up from the nap.

Immediately, I called Marco to let him know I was getting dressed and would then be heading down to the lobby area to meet him. Calling Neoshi back, she answered the phone like it had been ages since we last spoke. She was telling me we had so much to catch up on and so forth. I promised her we would link up for breakfast since I already told Marco I would be meeting him in the lobby. Although we came to Vegas together, my plan was to spend this time with Marco and then kick it with Neoshi when we did group activities only.

Instead of Marco meeting me in the lobby, he was posted up waiting for me when I walked off the elevators. When we locked eyes, he gave me a seductive smile reminding me of the dream I had just had, causing me to get a tingle between my thigh I wasn't expecting.

"How was your nap, Sleeping Beauty?" Marco questioned before kissing me on the forehead as he wrapped one arm around my waist and pulled me closer to him.

"It was everything. I ain't slept that good in I don't know how long. It didn't even feel like I was sleep for that long. The time difference must've caught up to me."

"We only been here for two days, so I'm sure that's what it is. Your body gotta adjust to the difference." I could smell liquor on Marco's breath, but he didn't seem to be drunk or slurring.

"Yeah that's what I was thinking. What you been doin, gambling the whole time?"

"Pretty much and drinking while waiting for your call." He replied as he grabbed my hand, and we proceeded to walk through the lobby area of our hotel which was also a casino.

"You wanna play some slots or something?"

"Yeah, I'mma try my luck. Normally, I'm not a gambler but I guess since we're in Vegas it's only right that I do."

"Ok, you lead the way." Taking lead, I headed to the first machine that caught my attention. The name of the slot was Lotus Land; it was the pretty white tiger that caught my eye at the top of the machine.

Putting my game card that was given to me upon our check in, I was ready to start my gambling antics. The game was a twenty-five cent machine but the minimum bet was two dollars, that part I never understood. Instead of trying to figure it out, I simply retrieved a fifty-dollar bill of my own money from my purse to insert.

"What you doing?" Marco interjected as he was handing me a blue face hundred-dollar bill when I turned to see what he was talking about.

"I was putting my money in so I could play. What you talking about?" I questioned him.

"Put your money away. I brought you to Vegas on my dime not yours. I respect the fact that you want to spend your own money, but I would've never told you this was my treat if I was going to decide when and what to pay for baby." I simply smiled at him and put my fifty dollars back into my purse before grabbing the hundred from his hand.

That hundred dollars actually went a longer way than I expected. We had been sitting at the same slot for over an hour and I was up five hundred and sixty-three dollars more than I started with. Every time I wanted to walk away, I would hit then get hooked right back.

"Ok, you better walkaway at five hundred even before you get consumed again." While sitting and playing the game Marco and I had drunk so many shots I lost count. That's probably the reason I was still sitting there.

"Oh, I am. Shit, if I would've walked away last time I hit I would have almost a thousand dollars." I complained before taking another sip from my cup.

"I thought you was gon' walk away then too but when you didn't I just let you do you. It's all about enjoying yourself."

"Yeah but that extra money would've been a bonus." I said and slapped my hand on the repeat bet button again.

Before I knew it, I was at an even five hundred dollars. I looked over at Marco and he started laughing as if he was reading my mind. I was torn between pressing cash out and repeat bet. Instead of taking a chance of going under the five hundred amount, I pressed cash out and grabbed my cup so we could walk away from that machine before I continued.

"It's your time now. I wanna watch you work and see what your luck looking like." I said as I wrapped my arm around Marcos as we walked though the casino.

"Hopefully, with you on my arm, I have more luck than I had earlier. I was up then turned around and lost it all."

Marco chose to play a game called Roulette. When we first got to the table, I was lost as to how the hell he was supposed to play. As time went by, I understood the basic concept of the game but not enough to put my money in on it. The minimum bet per time was twenty and that was too rich for my blood. Marco seemed to know what he was doing because he had been hitting since he started. When Marco realized he was up a couple thousand in chips he decided he had enough for the night.

"Looks like you are my good luck charm." Marco said as he wrapped his arms around my waist from behind, and we walked through the lobby.

"You're mine too." I slurred back to him.

"Don't just be saying that because I did."

"I'm not. You are. We both won." I was telling Marco the truth. I may have slurred and been a little drunk but it was the truth. They say a drunk speaks a sober mind.

"You wanna order room service or grab something from down here before we go back upstairs. I'm lit. I gotta grab something to soak some of this liquor up. Plus, we ain't ate since earlier, and it's almost two o'clock in the morning." Looking at my phone, I hadn't realized so much time passed while we were playing.

"We can grab something down here before we go upstairs." I said and pointed to the Mexican restaurant near the elevator.

We both order chicken tacos with a side of Mexican rice. Of course, Marco ordered extra tacos because the meal only came with three. The moment we got back to our room, I headed straight over to the balcony. For some reason, I just wanted to sit outside and enjoy the view of Vegas night life.

"You ain't hungry?" Marco came out on the balcony with a taco in hand.

"Yeah, I'mma eat. I just wanted to enjoy the view for a little bit."

"Oh ok." He said and walked back inside before returning with both of our food.

We ate our food as we looked at the heavy traffic and crowds of people walking the street as if it was evening instead of two in the morning. Once Marco finished his food, he headed inside for a shower. Considering I had already showered earlier, I didn't plan on getting back in until the morning.

While Marco showered, I poured myself a drink from the selection of liquor Marco purchased the first day we arrived. Of course, since I had been drinking dark while we were downstairs that's what I continued with. 1738 had always been one of my favorites but lately Hennessy VSOP has been my drink of choice.

I stumbled to change into my cute little nightgown before Marco finished up in the bathroom almost spilling my drink. Once I looked myself over in the mirror, I headed back out onto the balcony to await Marco.

"Damn, I wasn't expecting to see this when I came back." Marco said eyeing my body from head to toe as I sat in the lawn chair and sipped my drink with my legs crossed. Thank goodness we were on the twelfth floor. Nobody walking the sidewalk would be able to see that I didn't have any panties underneath my gown.

"I wasn't expecting to get this eye full either," I said before licking my lips while looking at his muscular chest, then the nice bulge in his boxer briefs. When Marco caught my eyes on his prize, he gripped it to adjust himself. I gave him a side smirk and looked back at the scenery.

"Let me go grab me a drink, too, so I can join you." Marco said and walked back into the room to retrieve his cup.

Seeing him come back to the balcony without a drink in his hand caused me to give him the side-eye.

"Where your drink?" I questioned.

"I drank it. I ain't bout to sip or take it slow. We in the room now. I don't care how quick that shit hit me." He responded before taking a seat in the chair next to me.

Marco turned my chair to face him slightly before grabbing my leg and resting it on his leg. I didn't resist or pull back because I never minded him touching on me. I just hadn't given the goods up yet. Using his strong hand to massage my leg, ankle, and foot relaxed my body something serious. It's like he was hitting all the erogenous zones without effort.

Marco

When I walked outside onto the balcony of our hotel room, I was caught off guard seeing Casanae with a silk night gown waiting for me. I mean I've saw her in cute little night clothes, but I guess the Hennessey had a nigga turned on. My first move of massaging her legs and feet only turned me on more. We had yet to be intimate in any way, so I honestly was scared to make the first move, but it was now or never.

Removing her legs from my lap, I stood from the chair immediately. Leaning down over her, I planted soft kisses starting at her forehead and made my way down to the nape of her neck. With every kiss, I felt her body relax a little more. Without resistance from her, I assumed that was my permission to continue and kiss further. When I started kissing on her chest above her breasts, I used my hands to roam down her body a little more.

Never been a nigga who was big on titties. I simply kissed around them and then headed straight for her honey spot. I raised her gown some only to see she wasn't wearing any panties. Pussy look like it was smiling at me when I came face to face with her other set of lips. Right there on the balcony, I slid my entire head between her legs and started using my tongue to part her pussy lips. Casanae spread her legs even wider allowing me full access. Propping her calves on my shoulders I made sure we were both comfortable before I continued.

I was hoping eating pussy was like riding a bike cause it had been years since I put my mouth on a woman in that way. From the movements and moans of Casanae, I wasn't doing too bad. Hearing the cars pass by along with the crowds beneath us only encouraged me more. It's not like they could get a good visual of what we were doing but the thought of others watching me, caused me to put on a show. Using my tongue to do all the tricks I thought would make her cream in my mouth, I caught myself letting out soft moans from the taste of her juices.

"Marco baby... baby... I'm cumming." Casanae moaned aloud. I begin to suck at her clit using my two fingers to penetrate her a little before I tried to make my next move. The cream from Casanae taste like some shit I wouldn't mind eating a couple of times a day.

"Marcooooooooo... Oh, my gawd!" She continued to moan as the juices spilled from her and into me. When she was done having her first orgasm I stood to my feet and picked Casanae up to carry her inside the room.

Laying her down gently on the bed, I begin to slowly remove her gown. As I removed her gown, she started pulling at my briefs. That motion on her end let me know, now was the time for us to finally take that final step. Both ass naked we both stopped and stared at each other's body in complete amazement. I leaned in to kiss Casanae on her lips for the first time and when she used her tongue to part my lips it was over with. As our tongues danced in each other's mouths, I gently eased my dick between her lower set of lips. Rubbing my dick up and down her slit, I get her body tense up some.

"You coo baby?" I questioned before I penetrated her.

"Um hum." She whimpered.

Pushing my dick inside of her slowly, I became a little weak in the knees. It's like her walls fit my dick perfectly. She wasn't too tight and for damn sure not loose. Although she was creamy as fuck, it seems to get wetter every time I stroked her.

I wanted to speed up my stroke, but the feeling was too good to rush the moment. Finally releasing my lips from hers, I planted kisses from her lips to the side of her neck while continuously stroking in and out of her. We were both moaning aloud and caressing each other's bodies with our hands. Casanae was digging her fingers in my lower back as I held onto her shoulder from under her arms as I started moving faster.

When I started plunging my dick inside of her harder, I felt her begin to fuck me back. When I felt she was able to keep up with my rhythm and pace I went in turbo mode. Fucking her faster and faster she was damn near screaming my name out in pleasure.

"Baby, this shit.. Man, this shit is perfect!" I moaned out.

"Marco, I want you! Oh, my Gawd, Marco, please don't stop. Don't stop!" She screamed out and little did she know I had no intentions on stopping. I had already nutted and we were on round two. Although I never once pulled out, I had learned that trick early on in life. Nut and get it right back up without your woman noticing and you can go all night.

When I felt her start to tremble some, I knew another orgasm was ahead. I started slow grinding her again before sitting up while continuing to still thrust in and out of her. Using my thumb, I starting moving it in a circular motion on her clit as I slowly watched my cream covered dick go in and out of her.

Just as I expected she started creaming uncontrollably causing my second nut to come quicker than I wanted. I continued to slow stroke until her orgasm was done and that's when I shot all my seeds inside of her. I know that's something we should've discussed prior but there was no turning back now. Hopefully, she don't be too pissed.

When I pulled my now limp dick out, her pussy started farting and making all types of noises. Damn near had me ready to dive right back in but I needed to make sure she was ready for that.

"Got damn it Marco!" She sighed as she wiped sweat from her forehead. I was so into the sex I didn't even realize we were both covered in sweat.

"What's wrong baby?" I questioned scared she was about to start spazzing out on me for nutting inside of her.

"Nothing bae, nothing at all. I just wasn't expecting all that." She said as she looked at me bashfully with a smile on her face.

"Shit, me either, but I'm happy it happened." I said before heading to the bathroom to get a washcloth. After lathering soap onto the small hand towel, I headed back to the bed where she was still laying down. She wasn't expecting me to wash her off.

"Bae what you doing?" Casanae questioned me as I parted her legs and begin to clean her off.

"I'm washing you off beautiful." I said as I continued to make sure all of the juices were wiped up for the most part. I wasn't trying to clean her completely. Just enough so she wouldn't be sticky between the legs. Once I felt my job was satisfactory, I returned to the bathroom to wash myself off.

"I know you ain't sleep that quick!" I said as I crawled into the bed next to Casanae.

"No bae, I'm just thinking."

"Bout what?" *Probably about that lashing I just put down!* I thought to myself.

"Whether or not I want to have another drink or not." She started giggling. All I could so was shake my head. This damn girl a mess.

"Want me to make you one. I was just thinking about making me another one. I done worked off that little drunk I had."

"You and me both. Well, I didn't do much work, but I feel like it." Little did she know that little pussy had enough power to do the work for us both.

Pouring a half of cup for the both of us, I knew how the rest of the night was about to go. Casanae sat up on the bed and took her shot to the head so I did the same and refilled our cups. The one thing I can say about Casanae is, no matter how drunk she gets, she still remains classy and doesn't get on any drunk shit. I don't mind drinking or kicking it with her for that reason alone. Some bitches you can chill with sober, but the moment they drunk they turn into a completely different person.

"Marco, we didn't use any protection, and I'm going to assume you nutted inside of me because you didn't pull out until we were done. Unless you didn't nut." Casanae said as she rolled over to look me in my eye.

"Nah baby, I won't even beat you up and lie to you. I definitely nut inside of you more than once. It was too good to pull out. Sorry baby, but I couldn't resist." I confessed.

"I guess I can take that as a compliment but…." I cut her off before she could ever finish her thoughts let alone her sentence.

"First thing it is for sure a compliment. Secondly, before you start thinking too hard, if my seeds actually work and something comes of this the choice is yours. I'm not saying I'm for abortions or anything like that, but whatever you wanna do I'll support. But I won't pay for it. I want you to be mine forever so take that as you want to."

"Yeah, let's not even have this talk right now. I don't even want to think about me as a mother right now in life. I'm not against having kids. Just didn't plan on it anytime soon. But if we ain't taking precautions then I can't complain. I don't believe in abortions so that's out the question for sure." I let out a soft sigh of relief because I would hate to have to pressure her into something she didn't want to do.

"Whenever you wanna talk about it, I'm going listen, just know that." I said as I pulled her in closer to me and held her tight as she nestled in my arms.

"Casanae? We crossed the line, and I honestly don't see myself going back now. I wanted you before we ever spoke, had sex, any of that. It's only natural for me to want you even more now."

"Ok, so what are you saying Marco?"

"Just a few minutes ago you were moaning out you wanted me. Did you mean that shit or did the dick have you talking out the side of your neck?" The time was now or never. I'm not no young ass boy who doesn't know what he wants so why perp like it?

"No, I meant it. I do want you. Although I meant that in more than one way at the moment, I can honestly say I want you too."

"Say less baby. You're mine now, ain't no reneging." I said before kissing her on her lips.

"No, you need to be telling yourself that."

"My mind is made up, Beautiful, and you are all I want." I said before closing my eyes to get some sleep before I found myself in between her legs again.

Neoshi

"Wait bitch, you did what?" Cassie questioned while laughing loud as hell. I had to look around to see who all was paying attention to our conversation.

"You heard me. I got up right before he was about to nut and ran out the room." I said before taking another bite of my breakfast as we sat in the Dunkin Donut's in the lobby of our hotel.

"What the fuck did he do?" Cassie was laughing so hard she could barely get her question out.

"Girl, his muthafuckin ass came chasing after me asshole naked and locked himself out the damn room. You ain't heard shit yet. Guest services had to come let him in because he locked the key inside the room when he came chasing after me."

"I'm surprised he ain't call Marco. I'm fuckin weak. I can't believe yawl." Cassie had tears running down her face from laughing so hard.

"He probably was too embarrassed, but I'm sure he gon' tell him when they get alone or back home. Shit, he had me fucked up. I was waiting for my moment to get his ass back for that disrespectful shit. Don't ever have me come to a fucking house your baby mom laid up in every night like some happy ass family."

"But they.." I cut Cassie off before she could even defend on Dave's behalf.

"I don't give a fuck if they were arguing, fighting or whatever; it's the principle. I don't know what the fuck they be doing midnight hours. Shit, as far as I'm concerned, they could be fucking on the nights we don't. Hell, he could've even kept it real with me and just told me she was living there, if that's what it is. And I emphasize IF cause we all know how niggas will lie through their teeth about fucking around with their baby mom. Whole time be in love with the bitch and never letting go but want to keep a bitch on the side. This ain't that and I had to let him know that." I fussed the same way I did when Dave called himself cussing me out for leaving him the way I did.

Just thinking about the situation pissed me off. When I broke up with my ex and started living my single life, I promised myself I would never allow another man to play me for a fool. So, I refused to allow it from Dave. Especially considering he ain't my nigga. That's just my dick.

"So, what you bout to do? Go upstairs and wake him up?"

"Yep. I'm ready to go shopping. He will sleep all day and party all night while we here if I let him."

"We supposed to go to the Wax Museum, but other than that we really ain't have nothing planned for the day. I wanna shop, too, but we decided we gon' go shopping our last day here."

"I guess that's smart, but I rather shop now cause between Dave getting drunk and my ass with these damn dispensaries we done spent most of our time here fucked up or fucking." I said and shrugged my shoulders.

"Wait, so you gave him some before that or after?" Cassie looked confused in the face as she waited for my response while I finished chewing the food that was already in my mouth before she questioned me.

"After girl. I ain't give him no pussy before that because I was too mad. But once I got it off my chest it was open season. You feel me?" I started laughing.

"You hell. That man gon' kick your ass. You better stop playing with Dave."

"He ain't gon' do shit but what I allow." I replied confidently. I knew I had Dave just where I wanted him and that's how it's going to remain until I say otherwise.

"Around what time yawl going shopping. I'm bout to head upstairs and get ready." Cassie said as she took the last bite of her breakfast sandwich.

"Probably about two. Shit, it's eleven now and Dave still sleep. Once I go back upstairs I'mma wake him up and he gon' take a good hour or two lounging around playing so it's safe to say closer to two o'clock."

"Lawd, I don't know what I would do with a nigga like Dave. That sleeping all day shit would aggravate the hell out of me. Like nigga, it's more to life than sleeping all day long."

"See, that's the thing. When we back home in Ohio, the nigga don't sleep half this much. He better not have that bitch pregnant again." I fussed while jumping to conclusions about him and his baby mom only pissing myself off. I didn't have any solid proof that they had been fucking around but I was almost certain that they had.

"Bitch, shut up. He could be tired for the jet lag still if he doesn't sleep like this when we home. That's how I was the first two days. I was beat. Marco wake up before me every morning, no matter how late he stay up the night before. I can bet he's upstairs fully dressed watching TV waiting on me to come get dressed."

"I bet he is too. That nigga is wrapped all the way around your finger. Just wait until he get a piece of that ass; it's really going to be over with." I joked. The look on Cassie's face told me she had finally given up the booty.

"Ohhhh, hell no, bitch. Spill the fuckin tea. I need all details!" I said eagerly as she tried to get up and walk away from the table.

"I'll catch you up on that at a later moment. Just know he's a keeper." Cassie said and gave me a wink before walking away in the direction of the elevators.

"Bitch!" I called out after her. She knew good and damn well she couldn't leave me hanging like that. Now I'm gon' be thirsty as hell for the details, and I gotta wait until she ready to tell me. I probably won't find out until we get all the way back home fucking around with Cassie.

As expected, Dave was still sleep when I walked into our room. I walked straight over to the balcony window and opened the curtain to let the bright sunlight take over our room. Dave flipped over instantly throwing the covers over his face attempting to block out the sun.

"Get your ass up Dave!"

"Give me thirty more minutes!" He said groggily.

"No, it's already almost noon. I been up since eight looking silly trying to find stuff to do without you so I wouldn't have to wake you." I complained as I rushed over to hit him with the pillow he was originally resting his head on.

"Come on Neoshi, man!" Dave fussed. I knew I was irritating him, but I didn't care. The most he was going to do is get his ass up.

"No, you come on." I said before climbing on the bed and beginning to jump causing too much motion for him to continue to sleep.

"Damn! I'm up! I'm Up!" Dave said as he sat up angrily on the edge of the bed rubbing his head.

"Now get dress hunny!" I said in an innocent voice as if I didn't just come in the room on a bunch of drama.

"Go start the shower water for me. I'm bout to get my morning cup in so I can get started before your ass piss me off." Dave said as he stood to stretch.

Dave

This Vegas trip been full of all types of shit. I definitely needed the break but I for sure saw another side of Neoshi, too, while we were vacationing. She ain't the sweet pea I thought her ass was, but she still ain't got shit on Nyia annoying ass. Neoshi just a brat fa real. Nothing a little dick can't change.

When Neoshi doesn't get her way or feels like things are about to turn in the direction she expects them to be heading she gets on her bullshit. For the most part, it be good bullshit except that little stunt she pulled the first night we fucked at the Hard Rock hotel. That shit was uncalled for and could've cause me some serious damage. I could've wrung her fucking neck. In all my years of fucking, I ain't never had a chick get up off the dick mid-bounce and bang out on me. I guess it's a first time for everything.

Nyia done blew my phone up every got damn day I been gone. Even with her on my block list she still finds another way to try to get through. Whether it's from her work phone or a fucking text app she been trying her best to get in contact with me. The moment I answer the phone and realize it's her I hang up on her ass. Ain't nothing that important to keep calling me while I'm supposed to be enjoying myself.

Before we left Ohio, I talked to Ross about checking up on my son and making sure he was to let me know if there was an emergency. As long as I talked to my brother every day, and he told me my little man was coo, there was no need for me to talk to Nyia. Of course, she don't see it that way. She never does. Originally, I wasn't going to tell Neoshi who it was blowing my phone up acting all possessive and shit, but after our situation I ain't have no choice. I wasn't about to stay in a hotel room with her miles away from home with a dry dick our entire stay.

I explained everything to Neoshi about Nyia and our situation. She wasn't too happy, but she didn't trip like I expected her to. Once I explained the type of woman Nyia was to her she seems to understand a little more but I could tell by the way our conversation went she wasn't going to tolerate me or Nyia disrespecting her so I nipped that calls in the bud.

BLOCK! That's exactly what each number Nyia called from would be getting. Better yet, the moment I get back home I'm putting her ass out. She thought she was about to keep lounging around my crib, but I had another thing coming for her ass.

Push comes to shove, if I have to go to court for my son then I'll do that. I'm not bout to tip-toe around my own house and life because I'm trying to avoid the crazy antics with Nyia. For all that, I might as well make her my woman again. That's not happening so she got to go. Plus, Neoshi will never be ok with Nyia living with me long term so she got to go. Neoshi didn't put a request or a date on when Nyia had to go but it's only common sense she ain't gon' to accept it much longer now that she knows.

"Neoshi, why don't you just marry a nigga and get it over with? I mean, we already in Vegas. They say what happens in Vegas stays in Vegas. We ain't gotta tell everybody till you ready!" I said to Neoshi as I slapped her ass while we walked the strip in route to our hotel.

"Shut the hell up. You say whatever comes to your mind, don't you? I mean, without any thought or consideration to it, huh?" She said as she continued to walk as if I ain't just ask her a question bitches would die to be asked.

"I'm serious as fuck. You mean to tell me you don't wanna get this dick the rest of your everlasting life?"

"That's your problem. You play too much. Ain't nobody stunting you Dave!"

"Damn, it's like that. You really just gon' brush my proposal off like it ain't shit. What I gotta do, huh?" I said as I got down on one knee in the middle of the sidewalk. "Neoshi will you be my wife?" I called out as she was still walking ahead of me not realizing what I was doing. When she tuned around and realized I was on bending knees in public she couldn't hold her laughter in.

"Dave get the fuck up now. NOW! Before I embarrass the shit out of us both." She said as she tried to pull me by my hand I had extended to hold hers.

"Ok ok, I quit!" I said as I stood up and brushed my knees off. "No, but seriously, why won't you be my woman Neoshi?" I had to get serious because I really wanted to know why she was avoiding being committed to me if she wasn't fucking around with no one else.

"It's not that I won't be your woman; it just that's not what I'm looking to get involved with right about now. When we first met Dave, I was fresh out of a long-term relationship that was trash. I got my heart broke, so I'm in no rush to commit again. I need time to heal completely from what he did to me before I start looking to start something new with someone new." Neoshi replied.

"I respect that. So, when you say commit to one person, I got a few questions. You fucking more than me?" I needed to know. If she didn't answer this shit right, I was leaving her right here in Vegas to find her own way home. I don't give a fuck if our tickets back to Columbus were paid for already or not. She wouldn't be flying back on my dime if another nigga was hitting that ass.

"No, I'm not fucking anyone besides you Dave. I mean, do you really think I would cuss you about about fucking around if that's what I was doing?" She looked at me as if I was asking some sort of stupid question.

"Ok, so if that's the case, technically, you are already committed to me just without the title. So, you saying that you need time makes no sense to me but whatever. You women confusing as fuck. Say yawl want one thing but then turn around and ask for another. Then when a nigga give yawl what you want it's the wrong thing. Fuck it. I give up." I said feeling defeated. There was no way I was going to win this debate, or her for that matter.

"It's not like that. I guess maybe I'm explaining it wrong to you. But I don't want a boyfriend right now. I'm happy with what we have right now. There's no disappointment or hurt when you only have the friend title. Soon as you give it a title that's when shit starts to fall apart. So, if it ain't broke I was always taught don't try to fix it. Leave well enough alone and we'll be fine. If we're meant to be together, we'll end up together. For now, let's just enjoy the moment and leave things how they are."

"You sound like a straight nigga that just gamed me the fuck up. Fuck this shit. I need a drink. I feel like you just threw me a pad for my draws." I said and left the conversation alone before she played me any weaker and a nigga pride got hurt.

Nyia

The first few days Dave was out of town I was torn between being happy and hurt. One minute, I was relieved we wouldn't be arguing all day and night, and happy that he trusted me enough to leave me in the house alone. Then, the next minute, my feelings were hurt that he left me and his son behind. I mean, we could've even found a babysitter for DJ and I went with him but no. He didn't even think to invite me along with them. I'm sure they down their meeting bitches and living their best lives. All these years put in with Dave and he has never taken me outside of I-270.

That's the only thing that kept me having a clear head while he was gone because I know Dave. Dave ain't about to pay for another chick to go on vacation with him so that was out of the question. Now when they got down their him fucking with some random bitch or kicking it with a bitch is a whole nother story. I know my baby dad and he's no trick but he's friendly with his dick for sure.

They were due to land last night for the information Ross gave me, but Dave didn't come home last night. I been at work wrecking my brain worried if he was ok or not or if Ross lied to me. Normally, Ross stays out of our business and doesn't pry, so I had no reason not to believe him. Marco didn't come home either which is what made me believe that there must've been a delay in their flight or something. I tried to call Dave but of course he still had my number on the block list. If I don't hear from him by the time I get off work today I'm calling Ross again to see if he has any updates.

My workday seemed to go by slow as hell. I was kind of relieved when my sister called and asked did I want her to get DJ. It's rare for DJ to leave from with me or Dave but with Dave gone for a week I needed this break. Instead of going straight home, I stopped by Walmart to pick up DJ a few items before my siter changed her mind. Once I grabbed all the essential things he would need to stay with my sister, I dropped his ass off and kept it pushing.

Pulling up to the house, I had intention on pulling in the driveway, but Marco's Audi was in the driveway. Dave's truck was nowhere in sight. The day they left they both took their cars, so I expected to see Dave's as well. Rushing out my car, I assumed that they had just got back so Dave would be arriving shortly. Deep down, I wanted to cuss him out, but I missed the hell out of him while they were gone, truthfully. I could play tough on the outside all I wanted but Dave knew how I really felt about his stupid ass.

Walking into the house, I was appalled by what I was faced with. Needless to say, Marco was comfortable chilling on the couch cuffed up with the same chick he brought by the house that day Dave and I were arguing. As bad as I wanted to question him on Dave's whereabouts, I didn't. I won't lie, seeing them shacked up all comfy made me uncomfortable as hell. It's not my house so there's nothing much I can say or do so I went straight to the basement without even speaking.

My mood went from sugar to shit in a matter of seconds. Grabbing my phone, I immediately scrolled to Dave's name in my contacts and called him. Unlike before, my call didn't go straight to voicemail so that meant I was off the block list. Why wouldn't he answer if he was no longer blocking me? *That only meant he was back in Ohio and would be returning home.* I thought to myself.

Hearing the alarm chime from a door opening, I assumed Marco opened the door for some reason until I heard Dave's voice. Something inside of me told me to rush upstairs but I decided against it. I'm sure Dave would make his way down here eventually.

Almost thirty minutes had went by before Dave finally walked down the stairs.

"What's up Nyia? We need to talk." Dave said.

"What's up? How was your trip, mini vacation, whatever you want to call it?"

"It was coo." Dave responded dryly.

"Ok, so what we need to talk about. You ain't asked for DJ or nothing." The fact he had been gone all that time and the first thing he is worried about is having a talk with me, pissed me off. Why was he not worried about the whereabouts of his son.

"DJ straight. I just stopped by Neeka and saw him." he replied catching me off guard. How the hell did he know where DJ was, and he hadn't even spoken to me since the day he left. I didn't call and tell Ross anything about me dropping DJ off, so how did he know? "Ain't no simple way for me to put this shit." Dave said and let out a deep sigh causing my eyebrows to raise.

"No easy way to put what? What you need to tell me? Dave, please don't tell me you got some bitch pregnant." My heart dropped to my fucking toes thinking about Dave having another child on the way by someone else. There was a lump in my throat, and it felt like somebody had just placed a hold on my heartbeat.

"Nah. Nah, that's not it." Dave said before letting out a chuckle. It was a relief hearing him say there was no baby on the way but still confusion.

"Ok, so what is that hard for you to tell me. Just say it." Any other time Dave come out and say what the fuck he wants, so what made this time any different?

"It ain't hard for me to tell you. It's how you gon' take it that's the hard part. It's time for you to move up outta here. I already paid Two Men and a Truck to move the stuff you got here out, but you gon' have to be responsible for the shit that's in storage to be moved. It's been more than enough time for you to get shit worked out on your end. I did my part as a father by allowing you to stay this long. I don't owe you nothing more, nothing less."

Instantly my face scrunched up. I couldn't believe how he was randomly coming at me about moving out. Then the nerve of him to say he did his part as a father. What about his part in my life? Like, I just don't get where he's coming from.

"Wait, what? So, you want me to just up and move out without any notice? Where are me and your son supposed to go? Where is all this shit coming from?" I felt my temper rising along with the tone of my voice. I was trying to keep calm so Marco and his company wouldn't hear us, but I couldn't keep coo.

"I don't need to give a notice when you living in my house expense free. When I say you gotta go, you gotta go. Plus, you originally said it was temporary but it look like to me you done got comfortable and looking for this to be long term and this ain't that. You gon' have to figure out what's going on with your place. Maybe this will help you to put some fire under their asses. I don't know no place that take this long to get a tenant moved in who already paid their first month's rent and deposit."

"Ok, so where is this shit coming from. This ain't something you just up and decided. You could've told me this shit before you left so I had some time. When do you expect us to be out by?" The mixture of hurt and pain was enraging me to a point I was ready to just start tearing shit up, Dave included.

"Today! You gotta get this shit outta here today. It's still early; ain't no excuse. You ain't got DJ, Neeka said he coo with her for the next few days so he won't be in the way." Dave said before turning to walk back up the stairs, and I charged after him raining blows in the back of his head and upper back.

"Ahhhh Bitch! Fuck is wrong with you?" Dave yelled as he turned to face me while I was still throwing punches. My arms were moving like a mad woman's trying to fuck him up. How dare he do me like this?

"Alright bitch, you better calm the fuck down for I hurt your silly ass in here." Dave yelled as he struggled to keep a grip of my wrist so I couldn't continue to fight him, but it wasn't enough. I started throwing my body against his and kicking my legs up attempting to kick him right in his dick. That's the thing that got me stuck with his sorry ass all this time anyways.

"Get the fuck off of me Dave. Get the fuck off of me!" I screamed. I guess all the commotion and yelling got Marco's attention because I heard him yelling for us to cut it out.

"Nah, this bitch tripping. If she don't calm down, I'mma fuck her up. I swear to God, on my son." Dave fussed and appeared to be out of breath just like I was from trying to fight him but that wasn't going to stop me. I calmed down some so he would think I was coo and he fell for it. The moment he let go of my wrist, I headbutted his ass right in the mouth.

"BITCH!" Dave yelled before back handing me so hard I flew back against the wall. Looking back at Dave, we made eye contact, and I saw someone I didn't know. He had never put his hand on me in a serous way. The most he's done is pushed me back or mugged my head, but to draw blood by back handing, this was a first. Placing my left hand to my mouth, I noticed it was bleeding heavier than I thought.

Rushing to the bathroom, blood spilled from my mouth into my hand. As hurt as my face was, I still wanted to fight some more. I wasn't done with Dave just yet. How could he do me like this? Talk about embarrassment. I should've known he would never change.

Marco

Talk about chaos; that's all it's been for the past twenty-four hours. If this is what it was like having a baby mom, I don't want it. Well shit, I don't want just a baby mom anyways. I want a wife. The shit Dave been going through since we got back would be enough to have my black ass back behind them steel bars. I ain't got the patience for a chick like Nyia to be permanently stuck in my life because of a child we share.

I knew he planned on putting Nyia out yesterday but I ain't know she was going to respond the way she did. Especially with Casanae being there, I thought she would try to remain a little more classy but she didn't. Dave did everything he was supposed to do as a man, but she was pushing my nigga to the fucking edge. Putting her hands on him and trying to tear shit up wasn't going to change his mind. If anything, it only made him want her to get gone even more.

After he back handed her ass, I thought he had knocked some sense into her but once she got her lip to stop bleeding, she came back for more. I didn't want to get involved, but I wasn't about to sit back and watch her try to tear up the crib I helped to pay for as well. The fighting between her and Dave I stayed out of because I knew he could handle her, but when it came to my property I couldn't sit back and watch. During the confrontation Casanae was upstairs in my room the entire time because I didn't want her to feel obligated to get involved on the strength of me.

It took us hours to get Nyia crazy ass out the fucking house. Dave and I had to physically carry her ass outside and run back in to lock her out. I told Dave to call the fucking police on her stupid ass before the neighbors did but he refused to. I ain't have shit to hide from the police and neither did he, but he was still against it. Normally, I ain't with adding the pigs to your business but there was no other way around this madness. If Nyia fucked around and called the police first, then they for damn sure would be taking Dave to jail. Whether it be for a domestic dispute or a domestic violence charge, they would find something to pin on him. That's just how the system worked.

After screaming, crying and banging on the doors for hours, she finally gave up when Neeka pulled up to get her. You would've thought a switch went off in Nyia's head when her sister arrived. The moment Neeka pulled up she stopped all the dramatics and got in the car with her as if nothing ever happened. Had we known she would bow out the way she did in the presence of her sister we would've been called Neeka. Dave ended up calling Neeka when I recommended for him to call the police. He told her that the law was about to get involved as a threat and she rushed to our crib to get her sister. The way Nyia acted in front of her sister as compared to when she wasn't around was awkward, but as long as she was gone I didn't put too much more thought into it.

Soon as the coast was clear, Dave called up the moving company he had paid to help her. Within an hour of Nyia being off our premises, all her shit was moved out. The nigga even went as far as having her car towed to her sister's house. He was beyond fed up, and I could tell just by the way he spoke her name. Once all Nyia's belongings were gone, Neoshi stopped by with perfect timing. I don't know if she came by to check on Dave or because Casanae told her about the drama taking place.

Dave ended up leaving and staying with Neoshi for the night but this morning when I got up, he was in the kitchen having a cup of Hennessy straight. Talking to him, I could tell he was under far too much stress all for a nothing ass bitch. That's exactly what Nyia is in my opinion. Nothing. Being concerned on how things were going to play out with DJ was all he kept mentioning. The only advise I could give him was to get a lawyer and go for joint custody. All he could do was shake his head and drink.

When it comes to children and the system, it can get real ugly before it gets any better. I hoped for the sake of my nephew they could get something figured out before he gets old enough to understand what's going on. Right now he's only one so he won't remember anything that goes on. The earlier the better in my opinion.

Until Dave figures out what he wants to do in this situation, it's best for me to stay out of it until he ask me to get involved.

Casanae called Neoshi since they were both off from work for another two days. Our little trip was only a week total but they both took off extra days. It's a good thing they did because coming home to deal with this type of situation would've been enough to have anybody call off of work.

Neoshi picked Casanae up and they took off to God knows where. That gave me a little free time to check in on the businesses and make sure everything was running smoothly in our absence.

When I arrived at the first laundry mat, I noticed that the manager we hired to run that particular location was outside pacing the sidewalk smoking a cig. I'm fine with smoke breaks and a relaxed working environment, but the chick looked stressed out.

"Hey, what's going on?" I said the moment I got out the car.

"Hey Marco. We got a problem sir. I didn't want to interrupt you two while yawl was on vacation, but thank God yawl are back. Is Dave on his way here too?" She started rambling off at the mouth, and I was a little lost as to why she was so anxious with concern in her voice.

"Slow down. What's the problem? What's going on. Ross was still here. Any concerns you had you know you can always contact him in our absence." I advised and I led the way to the office in the back of the building.

"Can I close this?"

"Yeah, that's coo." I said as I took a seat on the edge of my desk instead of in my chair. "Now what seems to be the issue?"

"Ok, so at first I thought I was just paranoid but after a few weeks of the same thing I realized it's not me. Then, last week while yawl were gone an unmarked car stayed in that lot across the street watching our building at least four hours a day. Then the icing was put on the cake when a young, White dude that was dressed up came here questioning about Dave. He wanted to speak with Dave and asked when would be a good time to catch him here. I told him I was unsure because Dave was out of town, but he came back yesterday and now there's another unmarked car sitting across the street in that lot." She was pacing the floor of the office as she told me everything.

"Ok, first thing's first, India, calm down. There's no reason for you to be worried. Everything we do here is legit. I'm curious as to why they are looking for Dave but after I go stop by the other two laundry mats I'll be back by here." I tried to calm her nerves some before leaving out of the office in route to the other two locations. I planned to stop by the two car washes once I made sure everything was ok at the laundry mats first.

Imagine how confused I was when I stopped by, not only both laundry mats, but by both car washes and the same shit. The manger over the other two laundry mats, Shasha, told me a similar story about an unmarked car watching and an unknown,

White man coming in questioning the whereabouts of, not only Dave but me as well. Then to find out the manager Denise who is over the car washes experienced something similar. The only difference there wasn't any unmarked car watching or an unknown man questioning her. She had a customer who came by three times a week and each time he was in an unmarked car. She said that he called her by name every time he came, but she never wears a name tag, so she was confused as to how he knew who she was specifically.

Instead of going back by to talk to India, I needed to talk to Dave about all this. I hadn't touched a damn thing illegal since I became a free man. There was no need for anybody even close to the legal system to be questioning a damn thing about me. Dave been walked away from legal activities, too, so this shit had my mind all over the place. I tried to call Dave, but his phone kept going to the voicemail.

I sent Casanae a quick text letting her know I would be by her crib once I hollered at Dave. I called up Ross and asked him to meet me at our crib because Ross is one of our silent partners. His name isn't on any of the buildings but he for sure helps invest so he in turn receives some of the profits. Anything revolving around the business he needs to be in the loop on.

Dave

They say when it rains it pours. That's exactly how I'm feeling right about now. Shit been hectic between Nyia and me since I put her out. The stupid bitch living with Neeka until she get her spot I guess. Neeka was on my side originally which is how DJ got to her house in the first place the day everything took place.

When we first got back from Vegas, instead of returning home, Marco and I both stayed away from home until I got my plan situated. Marco stayed at Casanae's and I stayed over to Neoshi's. I called Neeka up the next morning once I had taken care of the movers. When I offered Neeka a couple of hundred to keep DJ for a few days, I didn't think Nyia would end up needing to stay over there too.

After me and Nyia had our fight and Neeka had to come get Nyia she switched up on me. Now Neeka got me on her block list and ain't fucking with me. I don't know if she's upset with me over slapping her sister or the fact that her sister and nephew had to live with her and her four kids. Either way it goes that's what family supposed to be for, right? I mean, blocking me all because her stupid ass sister got her face slapped back, makes no sense to me. She deserved that back hand. She lucky I ain't do her worse than I did. As many damn punches she landed on the back of my head, she deserved at least a black eye. Then the fact the bitch head butted me in my fucking mouth and split my shit first, was more than deserving of a busted lip in return.

Nyia and Neeka not talking to me ain't the problem. The fact that Nyia trying to keep my son away from me is what's bothering me. I done even went as far as calling the daycare he goes to and the fucking secretary gon' tell me he no longer goes there. I highly doubt she got him moved that quick. All them bitches just been in cahoots together if you ask me.

Marco's advise about getting a lawyer involved is my only other option at this point. The fucked up part about me getting a lawyer involved right now is I'm scared I would be setting myself up for failure. Right when all this bullshit started happening with Nyia and me, Marco came at me about the Fed's watching our businesses. As much as I wanted to think it was a bunch of paranoia, I know damn well not to take the Feds as a joke.

When the Feds start letting it be known they are watching you, it's because they have just about enough information to come get you. Unlike the state, the feds will build a whole case then come get you when they know there is enough dirt to charge you and send your ass away for some time. It's like the moment I feel like my life is about to get better everything started taking a turn for the worse. Financially, I'm stable but not enough to take a fed case on. Then to think that Marco and Ross could be affected by it too only stressed me out even more.

Marco nor Ross knew exactly what was going on and I wanted to keep it that way. The less they knew the less they could be held accountable for. It's not like I was moving weight though our businesses so I knew they wouldn't be in no bullshit.

It's been a week since Marco had that talk with me about the Feds and things seemed to have died down. When I questioned India, Shasha, and Denise, all three said things seemed to have gone back to normal and that there were no more unmarked cars. Although that held to ease my nerves, I knew it was only a matter of time before they resurfaced.

Outside of spending time with Neoshi I haven't done much of shit. I've checked in on my businesses a few times but not half as much as I normally do. I haven't been in the mood to do shit honestly. It's like I'm laying low to get my mind right but I'm only driving myself crazy. I ain't used to sitting still the way I have been. I think even Neoshi getting tired of me being up under her ass; it's that bad.

"Have you ever played Toon Blast?" Neoshi questioned me as I was scrolling through my phone doing some online browsing. Normally, I'm not an online shopper but Neoshi got me hip. Lately, that's all I want to do is see what new shit is online to cop.

"Nah, I normally don't play too many games on my phone. That shit is childish. What you trying to say I'm childish?" I questioned.

"Shut up. You know you childish. That shouldn't have even been a question. But that's not what I'm saying. This damn game is actually fun. It's addictive as fuck though. I'm going warn you. I used to talk shit to Cassie about playing it all day until I tried it one time, and that's all it took. Now look at me." Neoshi said as she tapped the screen with her thumbs playing the game.

"Nah, I'm too coo for that shit. I need like a card game, not no damn blocks. I'll leave that shit for the ladies. How the fuck would I look playing some damn block game on my phone. Yeah, it's a no for me buddy!" I said while shaking my head no, as if she was paying me any attention.

"You too coo for everything leave it to your cool ass." Neoshi replied and threw one of the decorative pillows she was resting on at me.

"Oh, so you must wanna start a war in this bitch huh?" I said right before catching her off guard with a blow to the head from one of the bigger pillows on her bed.

"Daave!" She yelled. I followed up with another blow catching her off guard.

"Dave what? What's up? You tough right? Do something then. You ain't gon' do shit!" I started taunting her because I knew it would only make her retaliate.

"Stop before you make me lose my game, and I have to fuck you up in here. I'm telling you, you don't want these problems." Neoshi said as she flipped her hair over her shoulder while still playing her game.

"Ain't nobody scared of your little ass. What you gon' do? Bust a grape in a food fight?" Just as she looked at me probably to roll her eyes more than likely, I caught her smack dead in the middle of her face with a pillow.

"Dass it! I'm bout to fuck you up!" Neoshi said before standing on the bed and jumping on me.

That's one thing I can say about Neoshi that was a lot different from many girls I fucked with; she was a kid at heart too. When most chicks would take shit seriously or be offended, she come right back with the same type of energy. When I want to be childish and get on her nerves, she just gives me a dose of my own medicine. That's a lot more than what I can say about Nyia.

The pillow fight turned in to a full-blown water fight inside of Neoshi's crib. She ain't care about water being everywhere so neither did I. By the time we were wore out and tired, I was ready to just say fuck it and call a cleaning company to clean up our mess. Her little ass wore me out. She protested against the cleaning company of course and said we would straighten things up in the morning. Little did she know when she went to work, I was calling someone to clean this shit up.

"Roll over!" I whispered in Neoshi's ear.

"I thought you was tired babe?"

"I am but I'm never to tired to slide in between them thunder thighs." I said through chuckles.

"Oh, so you got jokes huh?" She questioned as she rolled over to face me.

"Nah baby. I'm just fucking with you. You know you thick as fuck boo!" I said before busting out into laughter. It wasn't that Neoshi wasn't thick, but she's so small, and the only thing on her big is her ass.

"Yeah ok! Keep being funny, see the next time you slide in between these thick thighs."

"All jokes aside Neoshi. I love you girl!"

"What? Dave, where did that come from? Don't start that gaming bullshit cause you think it's gon' get you some of this ass tonight."

"Nah, I'm serious. I don't know how or when but somehow you got me. I'm stuck! I really do love your ass. I been feeling this way for a little minute, but I guess I was waiting on the right time to tell you. What's the problem? You don't love a nigga back?" It was hard for me to confess my feelings, but with Neoshi I felt like I could be myself and keep it real with her.

"I'm not saying that. It's just hard to take you seriously when you play so damn much. Plus, we've never talked about love or our feelings so for you to say you love me out the blue, it caught me off guard. I never said I didn't love you. Of course, I care about you as a person and your well-being."

"Nah, you ain't bout to shut me down like that. Fuck is I care about you as a person supposed to mean? I didn't say I cared about you as a person. I said I loved you woman! The fuck did you hear?" She wasn't bout to play me like some weak ass nigga.

"I mean I love you, too, but I'm not in love with you Dave."

"Shit, I ain't in love with your ass either then. Fuck you!" I said and rolled over.

"Aww babe, you mad at me now?" Neoshi questioned as she planted soft kisses on the back of my neck.

"Nah, fuck that shit. Get off me. Take your flat booty ass to sleep and leave me alone!"

"Babe, but what if I told you I had a surprise for you?" She said as she reached around and gripped a hand full of my dick.

"What type of surprise?" I questioned.

"Wouldn't you like to know!" She replied as I felt her body lower on the bed. Neoshi hadn't sucked a nigga dick before so I was confused as to what the fuck she was doing until I felt her lips on the tip of my dick!

Casanae

All that time I was wasting making Marco wait and becoming his woman was the best thing that could've happened thus far. I have not one complaint about him. After being single for so long I think I became accustomed to being by myself and thinking love wasn't for me, but Marco has definitely caused me to have a change of heart.

He's nothing short of amazing. Every good quality I've ever wanted in a man he has. Over the time of us getting to know each other, he took note of all the things I liked and disliked, so now it only comes natural for him to be spot on with each and every detail.

Now that we are officially a couple, of course we have sex all the time. It's to the point I think we may have Dave and Neoshi's horny asses beat. I won't lie though. I can't get enough of my baby, and he can't get enough of me. Just thinking about him now had me ready to get off work so I could be in his arms.

Marco and I still live in separate households, but that doesn't stop us from being with each other every night. Some nights, I stay at his house and others, he's at mine. On the nights we aren't together, better believe I'm falling asleep on facetime with him. I be damned if I give another woman even the slightest opportunity to get her foot in the door. Not that I'm saying Marco would do such a thing, but I still have thoughts like any other woman in the back of my mind.

Finishing up my lunch, I decided to call Marco and see what he was doing before I clocked back in.

"What's up beautiful?" Marco always answered my call the very same way he did since the very first time I ever talked to him on the phone.

"Hey Bae! I'm finished with my lunch. I was just calling you before I clocked back in.

"Damn, that's how you treating me today? I get the last few minutes of your break. What if I wanted to talk to you longer?" Marco teased.

"Bae, don't be like that. I was hungry. I ain't want to be smacking all in your ear."

"I don' watched you swallow food whole. What makes you think I give a fuck about you smacking in my ear?"

"Shut up. I ain't never swallowed no food whole. Now you lying!" I laughed at his humor.

"Yeah ok. I know what I saw. You can lie all you want in front of your coworkers."

"I ain't lying in front of nobody goofy. I'm bout to clock back in, though bae, so I'll call you when I'm walking out of here."

"Ok beautiful. Don't work too hard."

"I wont baby. I'll talk to you in a few."

"Aight!" Just like that, we ended our call. That few minute phone call would be just enough to help me get through the remainder of my shift.

"Hey Casanae, I was looking for you. There was a delivery for you while you were gone to lunch." Lauren, an older, White lady said to me as she walked in my direction.

"I went to the main cafeteria today because I didn't pack my lunch. Is everything ok?"

"Yeah, everything is fine. You had these delivered. You're lucky we're friends or I would have kept them for myself." Lauren said as she reached around the nursing station and handed me a Love box from The Million Roses company. Instantly, tears filled my eyes.

"Aww, these are beautiful! Thanks Lauren!" I said to her while still covering my mouth in amazement.

"Oh, don't thank me missy. My salary isn't big enough to have got these for you!" She joked. I knew she hadn't purchased them, but thank you was the only thing I could think of saying. I knew who the box came from, none other than Marco.

"Whomever got you these loves you on a level I've never been loved. I'm about to go home and tell my husband he's been demoted to boyfriend level." Lauren joked as she walked down the hallway to finish her rounds.

Staring at my beautiful roses, I was amazed how much this man continued to top himself. I knew for a fact the flower arrangement cost him a couple of hundred dollars just because the individual roses are fifty plus dollars. Not saying I wasn't worth it, but I never thought anyone would buy me any.

Every time I walked past my flowers at the nurses' station, it made my day just a little bit better. Before I knew it, I was walking out of the hospital speed dialing Marco to show my gratitude.

"THANK YOU BABE!" I screamed into the phone the moment he answered my facetime.

"You're more than welcome, Beautiful! I'm glad you like them!"

"Like? I love them. I can't believe you got me these expensive flowers babe. I would've been thankful with some regular daisies. It's the thought that counts babe." I advised him. Although I had never asked Marco for anything; he's always more than willing to give me any and everything.

"The world is yours baby. I told you that. I just wanna see you smile. Your smile is priceless so whatever it takes to keep that smile on your face I'm gon' to do."

"Aww babe, don't make me cry. I'm already super emotional. I been all geeky since I got back from lunch and my co-worker handed them to me."

"You ain't gotta get emotional baby; this is us. As long as we together this is the type of treatment you're going to get. Nothing short of what you deserve."

"Where you at? I just wanna kiss your face!"

"I'm at the laundry mat out north. I'mma meet you at my crib. Call me when you headed there."

"I need to go home and shower and change first babe. I been in this damn hospital all day. I need a shower." I complained. No matter how much physical work I did in a day, I still have to shower soon as I get off work. It's so many germs in a hospital I refused to not at least feel like I washed off some of them before I carry on with my day.

"You can shower. Just put on one of my shirts and stay in the room until I get there. You don't need to get dressed or put on anything more. I'm coming straight home to eat that box!"

"Ok babe, I'm hanging up before you say anything else to me like that on facetime while you're at work." I immediately got embarrassed as if someone heard him talking dirty to me. I'm not gon' pretend like I didn't like it when he talked like that cause my kitty was for sure purring for him, but that's for my ear only not everyone else's.

"Nah, don't rush off the phone now. I mean what I said. Take your ass to the house. I'll be there in like twenty to thirty minutes, soon as I finish up here."

"Alright babe. I'll see you when you get there."

"Ok. Call or text me before I get there if you want me to grab something on the way."

"Nah, it's coo. I'mma cook something when I get there for us to eat. Just hurry up and get your butt there." I said and ended our call.

Cooking for Marco was something I actually enjoyed doing, but he barely allows me to, so tonight I'm gon' show my token of appreciation with a nice meal.

I rushed to Kroger's before I went to Marcos's because I knew like hell him and Dave wouldn't have all the groceries I needed to complete a meal. Neither of them niggas ever cook or barely stay home. I would be lucky to find the items that match besides liquor and their glasses.

Neoshi

"Wake up, Dave. Somebody at the door." I said as I shook him in attempt to wake him up.

"Fuck them. It's too early.!" Dave replied groggily.

"No, get the fuck up and see who it is. They been banging for about five minutes now." Right as I said that, whoever was outside begin ringing the doorbell constantly.

"MAN, WHAT THE FUCK?" Dave yelled as he tossed the covers off him and hopped out of bed mad as hell he was waken up.

Of course, I naturally got up with him and put a pair of his shorts on, so I could be nosey to see who the hell was at the door. "THIS BITCH GOTTA BE FUCKING KIDDING ME!" Dave fussed as I hit the bottom step.

Hurrying to see exactly what he was talking about, I stood next to him at the front bay window. My eyes grew big as a saucer when I realized it was a chick, who I assumed to be a bitch him or Marco was fucking, spray painting bright neon orange letters on the side of the garage. Thank goodness that Dave's truck was at my house and my car was outside or I'm sure she would have gone for that instead.

"What the fuck is she writing and who the fuck is she?" I questioned.

"That's Nyia dumb ass!" Dave replied informing me it was his baby mom, as he rushed to put on his Nike slides that were by the front door. "This stupid bitch gon' make me kill her man. It's too early for this shit!" He fussed.

I agreed; it *was* too early for the antics, but based off what all he has told me about her this is right up her alley. I'm just confused as to where she came from with this type of behavior when I know for a fact him and her were at odds. She hadn't even allowed him to see their son ever since they got into it when we got back from Vegas, and that was over a month ago.

Right as Dave walked outside, she was completing her fluorescent masterpiece. "HOE ASS DAVE" is what it read; all I could do was shake my head. Baby girl was butt hurt that he didn't want to fuck with her, but she was really starting to go out sad. At some point, you have to just walk away and be done with a nigga. You can't force a man to want to be with you, especially when you doing stupid ass shit like this for no cause.

I couldn't quite make out what the fuck they were saying because I took a seat on the couch and watched from afar. This type of situation doesn't involve me. Those are baby mom/baby dad problems, and Dave isn't my man, so I'm going to remain in my place until further notice.

Just as I thought Nyia was done, as she walked away, she kicked the shit out of my passenger side door. That's where I drew the line. She had me fucked up. Jumping up from the couch, I noticed that Dave looked back to see if I was still in the window paying attention before he rushed towards her slapping the fuck out of her from the side.

"Nah, I got this. That's my muthafuckin car she kicked. I ain't got shit to do with yawl's problems or her attitude." I was talking my shit as I walked out the house barefoot. Dave's oversized boxers I had rolled at the hip, and a tank without a bra. It had been years since I had to put hands on a bitch but today was bout to be that day.

Dave rushed in my direction attempting to deescalate the problem. I don't know if he was doing it to prevent any confrontation in front of his house or if he felt, because she was bigger than me, he was protecting me.

"Dave, move the fuck out my way!" I said while still fixed in a trance, never taking my eyes off of Nyia who was talking shit. I could see her lips and head moving, but I was so pissed I couldn't hear a word she said.

"Nah, I got this Neo. Go back in the house. I'mma handle her and I'mma pay for the damage. Dave tried to reason with me, but I wasn't hearing it. I guess Dave saying he would handle her and pay for the damage triggered something in Nyia because at the point she started kicking my shit repeatedly, like I was really going to let that ride.

Running around Dave, I was surprised at how quick I was able to reach Nyia. My right hook caught the bitch off guard, and the left followed up. Them blows were all face shots and continued until Dave lifted me off my feet and carried me as I wildly kicked trying to get down.

"Dave, put me the fuck down before I start punching you!" I screamed while still kicking wildly.

"Ma, calm down. You got her ass." I laughed. I don't know what the fuck he found funny.

"Let that bitch down so I can give her what she want." Nyia had the nerve to be talking shit but never even go the opportunity to get a blow in.

"Bitch, shut up. You ain't even pinch the bitch!" Dave of course had to have a comeback. "No disrespect babe!" Dave hurried to clarify what he had just said to Nyia.

"Man, put me the fuck down." I wasn't worried about him calling me a bitch. I still wanted more of Nyia.

"Neoshi, I ain't putting you down. You might as well calm the fuck down." Dave said as he walked back into the house with me still in the air, closing the door behind him.

When Dave closed the door, Nyia ran up on the door as if it was a person and started banging again. If only she had that same energy when I was just beating up her face.

"You should've just let me finish beating that bitch up. She ain't going nowhere." I complained as he finally put me down.

"That bitch is real-life delusional." Dave said as he walked into the kitchen and returned with a cup full of liquor as if it was seven in the evening instead of seven in the morning.

"You just gon' let her keep banging on the door. Like what if your neighbors hear her out their doing all that bullshit and call the   cops?
I questioned.

"That's her problem. They can call who they want but I ain't calling the boys to my crib for no weak ass baby mom. She'll get tired eventually. It's only so much knocking she can do before her arm gets tired." Dave shrugged and continued drinking his cup of liquor.

Marco's Audi pulled into the driveway, and I was hoping like hell Casanae didn't go to work and she would be stepping out the passenger side. Unfortunately, when Marco turned the car off and stepped out there was no Casanae. Marco was looking around in confusion when he realized it was Nyia outside the house banging on the door. When he reached the side of walkway where he saw the spray paint his entire facial expression changed.

I never seen Marco mad, but I'm sure the mood he was in was damn close. You could tell he was cussing Nyia the fuck out. She wasn't even saying shit back. I wish like hell I was outside just so I could hear exactly what he was saying to her.

"Marco here!" I announced to Dave, who was back in the kitchen refilling his cup like it was happy hour instead of early ass morning.

"Man, I hope this nigga don't call the fucking police!" Dave said as he tried to rush towards the front door. Just as I looked back in the direction of Marco, he was taking his phone from his ear.

From the looks of it, Marco must've called the police because Dave for sure looked defeated. Nyia started back at her shit the moment Dave turned around and yoked her ass up. I knew he was pissed off but that wasn't going to help the situation any.

Marco walked into the house cussing under his breath before giving me a head nod. I knew he was irritated to the max just because it was still early in the morning, and who expects to have to deal with something like this when they pull up at home?

Dave walked back inside shortly after Marco and slammed the door behind him. Instead of remaining in the living room and listening to Marco and Dave go back and forth about the Nyia and her antics, I went upstairs to Dave's room so I could call Casanae.

"Hey boo. What's up?" Cassie answered my call on the second ring.

"Hey boo. You at work? You clocked in yet?" I questioned her before I started my story and ended up being cut short.

"Yeah, I'm here. Marco dropped me off a little early so I could grab breakfast from the cafeteria. I been craving their damn French toast like hell and they only have it on Thursdays."

"Ok coo, so you got a little second to listen to this shit." I said before breaking down the story of what just happened.

"Damn it, I wish I would've been there. That bitch is bat-shit crazy over Dave. Fucked up thing is he don't even want her ass, and she ain't getting him back for sure acting all crazy. I don't know what she don't get. I would've left him alone after the things he said to her the first time I heard them arguing. It ain't like he ever sugar coated anything for her when I was around, so why is it so hard for her to get it through her head.

"I don't know, but at this point she tried to take it out on the wrong person and got pieced up real quick. She lucky Dave grabbed me cause I was ready to beat her ass until the cows came home." I vented to my best friend.

"Ok, text or call me if anything else happens. I'm about to clock in. We over staffed today so I may be getting off earlier than I'm supposed to.

"Ok, try to have a good day!"

"Yeah, and you try not to go to jail." Cassie joked before ending our call.

Just as she said that, Dave walked in the room fuming.

"You coo babe?" I questioned Dave as he was rumbling through his clothes looking for a shirt to put on.

"Nah, the fucking police downstairs at the damn door."

"Ok, just tell them what she did. Is she gone?" I couldn't understand for the life of me why he was so mad. Shit, the police needed to be called. It's obvious nothing else was making this damn girl leave. Maybe the police will talk some sense into her.

"Hell no she ain't gone. Ain't no telling what she out there lying to them about.

"DAVE!" Marco yelled from downstairs.

"HERE I COME!" Dave yelled back as he threw a wrinkled, white shirt over his head.

Nyia

I don't know why the fuck Dave thought I was about to sit back and allow him to live happily ever after with some random bitch. I put in too many years to accept the fact that he just replaced me like old socks or something. I'm not no punk bitch, nor am I scared to express how I feel so until he felt my wrath, I ain't have no intentions on calming the fuck down.

Ain't no wrath like a woman scorn, and he gon' feel every little bit of my pain. Neeka told me to just leave Dave alone and move on. That's the problem. People from the outside looking in think it's that easy and it's not. When a person gives their all to a man, it's hard to walk away with nothing. I believe Dave needs to feel the same hurt I feel inside.

I been keeping quiet and trying to figure shit out so I could move the fuck out of Neeka crib and into my own apartment. I moved in yesterday and this morning when I was headed to work something told me to ride passed Dave house. To my surprise, neither Marco car nor Dave's car was there, but it was a car in the driveway. It wasn't just any car; it was that same little red car I saw pull off from the house a couple of months back.

Meaning that there was a bitch inside, and not just any bitch; the same bitch he was sneaking around with when I lived there. Dave obviously trusted her because she was left inside their house is what I thought. Imagine my surprise when Dave came outside with no shirt and just some basketball shorts. That was all I needed to see to confirm my suspicions of him messing around with the girl.

Seeing how he came outside let me know she must've been inside and just as I assumed me kicking her car brought her the fuck outside like I wanted. I wanted her to see me. I wanted her to know Dave was rightfully mine. I wasn't expecting her to run up on me. She lucky I had the spray paint still in my hands or I would've whopped her ass flat the fuck out, no questions asked. That bitch was too small to think she could really hang with me. Dave must've known I would've torn her ass up, too, because he carried her away.

Now I do feel kind of bad for putting Marco in it once again. Then again, I don't because he is Dave's friend, not mine, and if you're not with me then you're against me. Marco threatened to call the police on me when he saw the shit I spray painted on their garage. I didn't give two fucks about the police being called because as far as I was concerned, I still lived there. I had mail going there and everything. It was my word against Dave's. Marco ended up not calling the police because Dave rushed outside to stop him, but someone had to because they sure showed up.

When the police arrived, of course, I was still sitting outside on their porch crying and angry at the world. More so angry at Dave for putting me through all this. I told the police that Dave was the one who blacked my eye as well as busted my lip. Dave never punched me, but he did slap me, and I honestly don't remember who did what to me because him and the bitch he had inside both put their hands on my face. Me being light skinned left evidence I didn't need to lie about.

Of course, it being a domestic dispute they needed to hear his side of the story. When Dave came outside to talk with the police, we were separated so I don't know what he told them. When I saw them placing handcuffs on him and placing him under arrest a smile crept upon my face. There were very few ways to hurt Dave but going to jail was one.

I wasn't sure if the domestic violence charges would stick or not but that was just what I needed to get the ball rolling. I'm sure Dave would try to reach out and have me drop the charges but I for damn sure don't plan on dropping a damn thing.

If he knew better, he would be calling that bitch he had at the house who stole on me. She better hope I never cross paths with her out in these streets or it's curtains for her little ass. She just don't know what she got herself involved in. Certain things you got to know your place and remain in it. When it comes to baby dad and baby mom confrontations, the side pieces is supposed to mind their fucking business. I don't give a fuck if I kicked her car or not. Dave told the bitch he would fix it so she should've left well enough alone. Hearing him even say that made me want to show my ass even more which is why I started kicking her piece of shit nonstop at that point.

"Hello." I answered the call from an unknown number.

"Aye Nyia, this Marco, I just talk to Dave on the free call they gave them. He ain't going to court until Monday for some stupid ass reason but they can't hold him after that if you drop the charges. They don't have no proof or anything else on him so it's basically your word against his." Taking the phone from my ear I looked at my phone screen as if he could see me looking at it crazily.

"Marco I'm not going downtown. I'm not going to show up, but I'm not dropping them either. If I go and tell them that I lied, then they just going to pick them up on me for falsifying a police report. They should drop them if I don't show up." I had no plans on dropping shit nor was I going to change my story.

"Yeah, but in that case, the state has the right to pick up the charges. I mean, you did vandalize our crib and his woman's car. The least you could do is drop the charges." Marco tried to reason with me, but it only pissed me off more hearing him refer to that bitch as Dave's woman.

"Listen, it sounds like this is more of her concern than mine at this point." I said and ended the call. At first, I was just going to tell Marco whatever he wanted to hear just to get him off the phone, but that last remark only set me right back off.

The nerve of that nigga to call me and try to get me to help Dave out. Like, why the hell would either of them think it would be even ok for me to be on his side when he clearly wasn't on

177

mine. It's clear Dave did what he wanted to do by fucking with that bitch over me.

If I could've put money on betting that Dave was about to call shortly after I would've. Seeing the local jail number appear on my screen I couldn't do shit but laugh. I declined his call so quick. I already knew what he wanted. Basically, to say the same thing Marco had just told me. Only thing is I'm so upset right now I don't want to hear his voice tone.

Sitting outside in the parking lot of my job, I contemplated whether or not I should've just called off instead of calling in late. Instead of going into the Alliance Data call center like any other day, I turned my car back on and sent Neeka a text. Neeka was my emergency contact so she was the person who originally told my job I would be in late due to being in the emergency room. I told her just to tell my job they would be keeping me instead of discharging.

It's best I didn't go into the job anyways. One black eye and a big ass busted lip was for sure about to draw attention to me. It's bad enough I'm already going in late. Instead of hopping on the freeway to go home and get some rest while DJ was at daycare after the morning, I just had a few other moves to make.

What you did, uh

Yeah you know I love you, but I can't forgive it

You could tell me stay, but I have to go

'Cause I would not expect someone to stay around

If I let them down, oh

Turning up the volume, I tried to drown out my thoughts with Mahalia "What You Did" the entire ride to my destination.

Dave

The last place I expected to land myself was behind some fucking bars. Especially over Nyia stupid ass. All this shit could have been avoided. I don't know what she can't get through her thick ass skull. If she wasn't willing to allow me to see my son how the fuck did she feel like she had the right to come over my house spazzing out like we were a couple.

Bad enough the stupid bitch spray painted all on the side of my garage, but she left a bunch of dents in Neoshi car too. Neoshi doesn't have anything to do with Nyia, nor has she ever even met her so why take out your frustration on her car. It ain't like Neoshi's car did anything to Nyia; it's a fucking car.

I ain't gon' lie, Neoshi surprised the fuck out of me when she ran up and pieced Nyia ass with a couple face shots. On the real, I thought Nyia would give it to Neo cause Neoshi so small but Nyia ain't even swing back. It's funny to me that Nyia didn't even raise a hand at Neoshi but be so quick to fight me, and I'm a man.

I called Marco on the free call they gave me because other than Nyia it was the only number I remembered by heart. I couldn't remember the last four digits to Neoshi's number, but Marco ended up giving it to me when I called. I needed to speak to Nyia first though because that bitch needed to be making her way downtown soon to drop these got damn charges.

They locked me up Thursday morning, it's only Saturday, and I feel like I done been locked up for a good six months. I don't want to call home or none of that. I'm just ready for Monday morning to come so I can get the fuck out of here. Even if Nyia decided to be petty and not drop the charges, Marco can at least bond me out. I'd rather fight a petty as DV case from outside of the jail than inside.

It's not like I have a extensive ass rap sheet or anything like that, so there's no reason I shouldn't be able to get out on my own recognizance or a bond.

"Hopkins! You have a visit!" I heard the guard yell my last name catching me a little of guard. I knew for damn sure Marco wasn't coming to visit me. Nyia, on the other hand, would try to be funny by racing down here to see me just to make sure that Neoshi wouldn't be able to. Rushing off my bunk, all the things I wanted to say to Nyia came to mind. As bad as I wanted to choke her out the game, I had to remain levelheaded in order for her to cooperate with what I wanted her to do.

Walking into the small ass visiting area where I was closed in a two by two cell only big enough for myself, I was happy to see Neoshi's face on the other side of the glass. Picking up the phone receiver, I wipe it off on my shirt before placing it to my ear.

"What's up baby?"

"Hey babe!"

"What's going on. I wasn't expecting nobody to come see me. I ain't even know today was a visiting day for me."

"Yeah, I would've come on the first day you were here if they didn't have assigned days. I called Marco to see if he was coming first before I came down here, but he said he wasn't. He said to tell you to call his phone because he needed to holla at you about something important regarding the business."

"Ok, I'll call him after our visit. What he saying about that bitch Nyia?"

"I don't know; he ain't say nothing about her since Thursday when you first called him. I guess he called her and asked her to come drop the charges and she spazzed out and told him it was my concern not hers. I don't know, the bitch got to be slow or something. I don't get it."

"Hell yeah, I think her momma must've smoked crack or something when she was pregnant cause the bitch definitely ain't got em all. She ain't even dealing with a half of deck of cards let alone a full deck."

"I don't know how you dealt with her this long. She's just flat out stupid. Like, come on now, all this could've been avoided." Neoshi said while shaking her head in disbelief.

"That's my thoughts exactly. This don't make no sense. I ain't got no business being behind bars. Then she lied talking about I beat her up so they thinking them bruises came from me. I never even punched that bitch. She was just too embarrassed to tell the truth." I said and Neoshi started laughing.

We both knew who did what to Nyia's face, but I wasn't going to come out and say it while in here. I ain't know if they was recording or paying attention. I ain't have time for Neoshi to be catching a charge because we in here running our mouths too much.

"I been driving your truck. I hope that's ok. I wanted to ask you, but you never called me. Nor did you call Marco back. Marco put my car in the shop on Friday to get those dents removed so I was car-less and didn't have any other option."

"Nah that's coo. It's would've been the same way if I was home. Really don't make a difference to me if you drove my truck or if I drove you around in it."

"Two minutes! Wrap it up!" The guard called out letting us know the visits would be coming to an end in the next two minutes.

"Damn, these damn visits just as short as their punk ass phone calls."

"I know. I was expecting to at least be able to talk to you a little longer." Neoshi complained with sadness in her eyes.

"Don't worry baby. Daddy be home real soon." I joked.

"Babe, hush. Your mind in the gutter as always."

"You damn right, but nah, I'm serious. I'm gon' call Marco and see what he talking about then I'll call you later. You can put some money on the phone but not too much cause I only got two more days. Hell, not even that if they let me out early on Monday." Monday couldn't get here quick enough. That's all I kept reminding myself. Court was Monday, and I would at least be able to get home.

"Ok babe. Make sure you call babe."

"I will, I promise. I love you!"

"I love you, too, Dave!" Neoshi replied before hanging up the receiver she was holding in her hand. This was the second time ever I had told her I loved her, and I meant it more now than ever.

Marco

Something told me when the Feds came in the laundry mat early Monday morning it was about to be some drama. Since the very first time that India had ever mentioned them snooping around I had yet to hear anything about them. I thought we had nothing to worry about since the businesses were legit, but I guess not. I dropped Casanae off at work and stopped by to grab some paperwork to prove ownership of the business in case I needed it for court with Dave, and I be damned if I wasn't stopped in my tracks.

Being an ex-felon, of course when they barged in the building it scared the fuck out of me. I didn't know if they were going to pop a nigga or arrest me. Either way, I didn't deserve nothing they had to offer so a nigga nerves were bad. They gave me some paper about closing the business until their investigation was over with. They questioned me as to whom I was and my connection to Dave, but I didn't have any answers for them besides I was co-owner of the business.

Knowing I needed a lawyer present or else they would twist up my words I kept it brief with them. Once they handed me a stack of paperwork that I had no clue what meant, I rushed out the building leaving them there and headed over to the other laundry mat only to see it surrounded by the Feds as well. Instead of even going to the car wash, I headed straight downtown. Before I could get off the freeway at my exit, I had a text from Denise, the manager of the carwashes telling me it was an emergency, and I needed to get to there now. I already knew that meant they had hit that business as well.

I sent Denise a reply text telling her I would handle it after I left court with Dave. Never in my life had I been so nervous for absolutely no reasoning. Calling up the only lawyer I could think of to help me with this situation, I started thinking of all the possibilities the Feds could be digging into our businesses.

"Jerry speaking!" Mr. Thompson answered the call on the first ring.

"Hey Mr. Thompson, it's Marco Elliot. I need you man."

"How's it going, Mr. Elliot. I haven't heard from you in some time. How's life treating you? Judging from this random call, I take it you aren't staying out the way." He replied judging me off of my past and what he knew of the things I used to get involved with.

"Actually, that's why I'm calling you. I've steered clear of any legal troubles, so I thought. I ain't been doing much of nothing besides running my business and laying low under my woman in the crib. But see, Dave baby mom got him locked up on some DV lies and then the Feds came to our businesses this morning shutting them down until they complete some investigation. They closed both laundry mats and both car washes. I got some papers, but I don't know what none of this shit mean."

"Whoa, slow down Mr. Elliot. What does Mr. Hopkins... Dave's last name is Hopkins, correct?"

"Yeah, it's Hopkins."

"What does Mr. Hopkins DV charge have to do with the Federal courts. That's State level, and a misdemeanor at that. Let me look him up really quick to see what they are saying. Have you spoken with Mr. Hopkins since he's been detained?"

"Nah, I talk to him the first day he was in there, but I missed his call on Saturday. I was headed downtown now to go to his court appearance so I could get him out, but all this shit with the businesses and Feds threw me off so I called you first."

"Well, it's a good thing you did call. The Feds are digging into something a lot bigger than his DV case. It looks like the DV charge is going to be dismissed but they have a holder on him. He'll go before a judge this morning, but he will not be released. He's being held on a Money Laundering charge which is a federal crime. The state no longer has any control over what's going on with him."

"Wait what? A money laundering charger? But those are our businesses and that's our money. I mean, I know back in the day we did our little one two, but this money is clean money. Dave ain't guilty of that shit and I know it."

"I wouldn't be so sure. I can't really look into anything because when the Feds are investigating something, those files are encrypted and I'm unable to see them until they have completely built their case and it's listed in the dockets. This is something they are still working on. Normally, when the Feds start showing their faces, they already have what they need to get the conviction they want. I would talk with Mr. Hopkins if I were you, but that's going to be pretty difficult considering where he's at. I just searched your name and you don't appear to have anything on you as of now. But I wouldn't be too confident. If you guys are business partners, then nine times out of ten, whatever falls back on him will fall back on you as well."

My mind went blank because I was clueless as to how the hell a domestic violence charge turned into a money laundering charge that quick. If Dave was laundering money, he would've told me. There was no need for him to launder any money; all of the businesses were doing good. We weren't rich but we were comfortable. Comfortable enough to leave the illegal shit alone.

"Thanks, Mr. Thompson. Is it coo for me to bring the paperwork they gave me to you for you to look over. I also wanna drop some money off as a retainer in case we need your help with these cases."

"No problem. Yeah sure, you can drop the paperwork and money off. Do you know where my new office is located?"

"Nah, I know it's near third, but I'm not sure the exact building." My line beeped; it was Casanae, but I would have to call her back once I finished talking to the lawyer.

"Yeah, I'm on the corner of Third and Main. The address is 100 East Main Street. You shouldn't miss it."

"Coo, I'll be there in like three minutes. I'm right up the street."

"See ya soon." Ending the call with Mr. Thompson, instead of calling Casanae back I needed to get in touch with Ross. Calling Ross, I wasn't too sure of how deep we were into everything going on, so I was hesitant about talking with him over the phone.

"What's up brah? What's going on with Dave. What they say? They gon' let him out on his on recog, or they gon' drop the charges?" Ross questioned the outcome of Dave's court appearance this morning with the assumptions of what would've been the outcome. Had the fed case not been pending, one of the two options Ross expected to happen would have happened.

"Hell nah. They holding him on some Fed case. I ain't even make it to the court appearance. I know they always start late so I stopped by one of the laundry mats and the big boys came in and shut shit down. I spoke with Mr. Thompson. I'm headed to his office now. From what he just said over the phone, shit ain't looking too good. But I don't know who all it involved besides Dave. Which makes no sense cause Dave's hands been clean for years."

"FUCK! FUCK man!" Ross yelled into the phone. "I'm bout to meet you there. I need to know that the fuck going on. And who all they trying to include in this bullshit."

"Bet, I'll holla at you more when you get here. I just pulled up." I said before ending our call.

I decided to call Casanae back before I headed into Mr. Thompson's office.

"What up, Beautiful? I was on the other line with the lawyer when you called. I'm sorry about that." I told her as I stared at her awaiting her response.

"Bae, what's going on. Neo called me going off about Dave not getting out and not knowing what's going on. She said they dropped the charges but didn't let him go for some kind of hold."

"Baby, I'm up here at the lawyer's office now trying to figure out what the hell going on. Soon as I leave here, I'll have more information for you. Call her back and tell her when Dave call tell him to call me asap."

"Ok bae. Are you ok?"

"I don't know just yet, but I'm going to talk to you more in person. I don't want to do too much talking on these phones."

"Ok, I'm bout to leave work. I'll be at my house. Just come by when you leave there."

"What you leaving work for? You alright?"

"I don't feel good. I threw up my breakfast. I think they ain't cook them sausages all the way or something." She said with her nose turned up.

"Probably not. I told you bout eating that hospital food. That shit ain't right. Text me if you need me to bring you something on my way there. I'm bout to run in here. Ross just pulled up."

"Ok bae." We ended our call, and I prepared myself for all of what Mr. Thompson was about to say.

Casanae

What the fuck am I going to do? I said aloud to myself. I begin to pace the floor of my bedroom. I don't even know where to start. First, all this drama and mess with Dave. Then the Feds closing their businesses. Now this, I can't handle too much more in so little time. I don't even know if I can be happy about this situation.

Looking at the Clearblue pregnancy test sitting on my dresser, I was in complete disbelief at the positive reading. There couldn't be a worse time to get pregnant than now. Marco is the perfect boyfriend, and I have no doubt that he will be an even greater father, but the question is will he be an active father. With all this Fed shit going on, who's to say he'll be here with me to be a part of this child's life.

Marco was the one who bought the pregnancy test because I been having too many symptoms. I honestly hadn't paid any attention to the symptoms I was having. When I did have pregnancy symptoms I never once thought to associate them with pregnancy though. That was the furthest thing from my mind, which I don't know why it was because Marco and I have never used any form of protection since we started having sex.

I never really keep track of my periods, only making matters worse. My periods are never regular so when they come, they come. If they don't, then oh well too. As bad as I wanted to wake up from this dream this was now my reality and I needed to see just how far along I was before I stressed myself out anymore.

Grabbing my phone, I immediately called Neo. I needed my best friend here with me.

"Neo? I need you!" I said fighting back tears.

"What's wrong with you bitch? I'm the one need somebody. Shit, my in-house dick been gone almost two weeks, and I'm over here going through it. Don't know when he going be free, and I'm sick of playing with myself."

"Bitch, that was so selfish. You worried about his dick and that man locked behind bars fighting for his freedom.

"Oh, trust me, Dave head on the same shit mine is. He knows I'm over here going through it. We have phone sex at least twice a day. Well, I have phone sex with him. He basically listens to me playing with myself. I don't know what the hell he be in there doing but I'm sick of it already."

"Eww, I don't wanna hear no more. Can you just come over here. I need my best friend?" I asked her to come over because I honestly needed her to comfort me.

"For what? Where the hell is Marco ass? It ain't like he at work." No matter the situation, I can always expect Neo to say some shit that just comes out all wrong.

"He ran over to Ross house to talk with him. I don't know when he plans on coming back, and I want my best friend, not my man bitch. Just come over here. You ain't doing nothing no way besides lounging around." I'd much rather show Noe the test instead of telling her over the phone. I'm sure her excitement will cheer me up some. Cause right now all I feel is fear.

"Oh, hush you big ass baby. I'll be over there in a minute." Neo said and hung up in my face.

"Beautiful? Where you at?" Marco called out as he walked into my house. I had just recently given him a key, and he has no problem using it. I jumped up from the cris cross apple sauce sitting position I was in on the floor and rushed to my dresser where the pregnancy test was laying.

Looking around the room, I got all paranoid as if he didn't know I was taking the test.

"Baby? Where you at?" Marco questioned when I didn't respond to him calling me the first time.

"I'm. I'm up here in the room bae." I stuttered a little nervous of his reaction to the news he was about to be faced with.

"Why you ain't answer the first time I called you. What you up here doing?" Marco questioned as he walked into my bedroom.

"Bae...." With the pregnancy test in hand, I was cut off by banging on the door.

"Who the fuck banging on your got damn door like that?" Marco's face scrunched up as he turned to go answer the door.

"Casanae get down here." I could hear the urgency in his voice, so I rushed to see what the problem was. I was sure it was just Neoshi since I had just called her to come over.

"MARCO ELLIOT, COME OUT WITH YOUR HANDS UP!" I heard an unfamiliar voice yell from the opposite side of the door. "WE KNOW YOU'RE IN HERE. MARCO OPEN THE DOOR OR WE'RE COMING IN!

Frozen in my tracks, I didn't know how to respond. Pregnancy test in one hand and my phone in the other, I was startled when they started banging on the door at the same time my phone rang. Jumping, I accidently answered the phone for Neo's call.

"BITCH, what the fuck is going on at your house. It's SWAT every fucking where and they got your whole building surrounded. Where is Marco? You better-" I ended the call before she could say any more.

"Beautiful, I'm bout to open this door before they kick this bitch down. First, what were you about to tell me?" Marco questioned with a worried expression written all over his face. With tears filling my eyes to the point I could no longer hold back from crying, I looked down at the pregnancy test in my hand.

"Bae, I'm pregnant!"

BOOM! BOOM!

Just as Marco said, they knocked my door off the hedges with just two big ass bangs. Rushing in my house, two officers threw Marco to the ground while several others filled my house with guns drawn looking to see if anyone else was inside.

Nothing to say and numb to what the hell was going on, I watched as they handcuffed the father of my unborn child in the middle of my living room. When they read Marco his Miranda rights, and he mouthed to me "I Love You!", my heart shattered in even more pieces because I did not want this to be our fate.

"I love you, too, Marco!" I said as they escorted him out of my house. They didn't explain anything to me or even apologize for busting my door down.

How did they even know he was here? All types of questions were flooding my mind as Neoshi rushed though the opening that should've been my front door.

"Oh, my goodness, boo, are you ok. I thought Marco was gone. Why did they come here for him? What did they take him for? Why yawl ain't answer the door?" Neoshi started rambling off questions, and I couldn't even give her any of the answers she was looking for because I was just as lost as she was. I simply handed her the pregnancy test and threw myself onto my couch. With my head in my hands, I cried my eyes out.

Neoshi

Had I known what I know now I still can't say I would've walked away from Dave when he initially started trying to fuck with me. Dave was a real nigga and I respect everything about him, behind bars or not. Now I can say he pulled others into his bullshit innocently, but I don't think that was ever his aim.

When Marco got arrested, it was merely on the facts that him and Dave were business partners, so he was legit guilty by association. Unlike Dave, Marco made sure their lawyer contacted Casanae first thing after his court appearance he basically forbade her from going to. Their lawyer informed Casanae that Marco wasn't being held on the same charges as Dave because Dave had come clean and told his lawyer as well as the detectives that Marco had nothing to do with any of the money laundering. Considering Marco wasn't being held on those charges, the charges they did have on him wouldn't stick so he could be released any day.

The only problem with that is the fed operate a lot differently than the state so until the lawyer calls Cassie back we are in the dark.

Of course, I was confused as hell where money laundering came from because this was the first time I had heard anything about it. Marco, Dave and Ross were doing a good job by keeping us women out of what was going on whether they were innocent or not. To my understanding, Dave was doing all the laundering under Ross and Marco's noses. They didn't even have the slightest clue that he was still into illegal shit after all those years of being clean.

Dave is looking at football numbers. Not no little shit either; the first number they threw at him was twenty years. The lawyer told Cassie that they always start high and work their way down, but he would for sure do at least ten if he didn't cooperate with them. I knew he wouldn't just because he's not that type of dude. I prayed not only for the sake of his freedom but for his son that he worked something out so he wouldn't have to sit behind bars all them years. That little boy needs his dad in his life, especially having a mother like Nyia.

As a friend, I'll always be in his corner, but we never made any type of commitment, and I'm thankful we didn't. I don't know if he expected me to ride this out with him but no woman in her right mind would. I love him but ain't no love that got damn strong.

Here I was feeling sorry for myself when Dave first got locked up and my best friend is going through it the most. On top of her man actually being innocent, she got evicted from her condo because of the swat incident, and she's pregnant. There's nothing I can say at this point to make her feel better.

"Cassie, you hungry?" I walked into the living room where she was balled up on the couch in a fetal position.

"No, I'm fine." She dryly replied.

"You gotta eat something. You can't sit around here not taking any vitamins or eating and expect that baby to make it. I know you don't want to hear it, but you can't let go of yourself like this." Looking at her broke my heart. Seeing Cassie down bad like this was a first. She was more than heartbroken and the fact that she was pregnant wasn't doing anything besides tearing her down even more.

"I don't feel like eating Neo. I ain't gon' do shit but throw it back up. So, to prevent myself from going through the pain of that I'm not going to force myself to eat. I'll eat something later when my stomach feels better." I knew she was lying because she hadn't barely eaten since the day they took Marco and that was almost a month ago.

"Ok, I'm going to make you some homemade chicken noodle soup. Last time that seemed to stay down pretty good. Just promise me you'll try to eat at least one bowl of it later." I had no other option besides to reason with her because me forcing her wasn't an option.

"I will." She replied and turned her head in the opposite direction attempting to get comfortable.

Walking back into the kitchen, I heard a knock on the door and turned in my tracks. Ever since the situation with the feds I been paranoid as hell, and I refuse to let them kick in my door. I can't afford to be put out my apartment. Where the hell would Cassie and me go then? Ain't no way in hell we bout to go live in

Marco and Dave's house. I don't care how many times Marco advised Cassie to go stay there; it wouldn't be the same without them there.

"WHO IS IT?" I yelled as I tried to look through my peephole to see who was outside my door unannounced. Seeing what looked like Ross' face I immediately opened the door.

"What's up Ross?" I greeted him with confusion written all over my face because normally he calls. Popping up ain't normally how he operates.

"Nothing much. How you ladies holding up?" Ross questioned as he walked inside and eyes Cassie laying on the couch looking defeated by life.

"As to be expected for Cassie." I replied pointing over at her.

"Well, I got some news for yawl. Yawl want the good or the bad first?" Ross questioned basically brushing off the fact that Cassie was laid on my couch looking like she was half dead but staring at him as he spoke.

"Shit does it even matter at this point. We keep getting hit back to back with bad news. I mean, either way you tell us, we gotta hear both, so you pick." I replied. We were in a damned if you do and damned if you don't type of situation.

Ross reached in his pocket and pulled out his phone before pressing a few buttons and connecting himself to a call. All he said was yep and ended the call, confusing the hell out of me even more. Within seconds my front door was opening behind Ross and he turned as if he was expecting a visitor. I, on the other hand, started walking toward the door. I had taken too many losses, and I refused for some random to just be walking into my house without being invited inside.

"OH MY GOD!" I screamed as Marco walked completely through my front door looking like he hadn't had a hair cut in years.

Marco rushed over to the couch where Cassie was laying and wrapped his arms around her as he whispered into her ear. Cassie was speechless as tears spilled from her eyes. I could tell she was in shock and trying to take in what the hell was going on because I was baffled at to how the hell and what the hell Ross was about to tell us next.

"What. When. How.?" I couldn't even get the correct question out. I needed answers and quick. I knew they weren't going to hold Marco forever, but I wasn't expecting him to come home anytime some. As much as Cassie needed him, I was confused.

"I'll leave that for Marco to explain to yawl." Ross said as he placed his phone back inside of his pocket.

"So, I take it this is the good news. So, go ahead and lay it on us. What's the bad news?" I questioned ready for whatever blow he was about to hit us with. I wasn't trying to ruin the mood with Marcos' grand appearance, but I needed to know what was next to come.

"Yeah, this is the good news. The bad news is Dave refuses to work out a deal and signed a plea deal this morning for twelve years. The only good thing about the feds is he don't have to do the whole twelve years. As long as he stays out the way he can serve ten months and it be equal to a year so its more like nine and a half years. It's still a lot of time but much better than a twenty ball."

"DAMN, that's fucked up!" I said and headed back to the kitchen. I couldn't lie; hearing that Dave would be gone for ten years basically hurt. Together or not, that had become my boo and damn near one of my best friends in such a short period of time. I can't believe he wouldn't tell me that he was going to accept a deal like that. I had just spoke with him last week and he told me if he had to make any serious decisions, he would tell me about it first. I guess he had a change of plans on that promise.

"Nah, you ain't heard the fucked-up part of everything. The fucked up part is that Nyia is the one who worked with the Feds to take Dave down. I don't know how the fuck she knew what was going on if me and Marco didn't even have a clue, but she knew too much."

"WHAT?" Cassie questioned. That was the first thing I heard her say since they arrived.

"Yeah, you heard me right!" Ross replied. The last bottle of Hennessy VSOP Dave got, I cracked open and poured myself a cup. I planned to keep it but after hearing that news I needed something strong. Walking back in with my cup in hand my mind was all over the place.

"Calm down beautiful. I don't need you worried any more than you have been." Marco tried to comfort Cassie as she tried to sit up on the couch.

"I can't accept that! I can't! I won't! She gotta go!" I said before grabbing my keys and walking out the front door leaving them all standing there curious on my next move!

THE END!

If you haven't already, make sure you check out other work by Chanique J:

No Love Given 1-4

Crazy About Your Love 1-2

No We With Without You and I 1-2

Loving Everything About My Savage 1-2

I Need You Bad (Standalone)

His Weekend Lover; Loving a Boss Through It All

Giving My Heart and Soul to the Realist (Spin-off of weekend lover)

A Street Queen Stole My Heart 1-2 (Collab with Tyanna C.)

When a Thug Pays You in Tears (Standalone)

Mob Life 1-2

Forever His Lady: The Charm of a BBW

Losing My Life at the Altar: A Domestic Affair (Novella)

Kinky Christmas Tales: Making the Naughty List (Novella)

Sleeping with the Assassin (Standalone)

Loving the Wrong Person All the Right Ways (Novella)

Made in the USA
Middletown, DE
14 October 2023

40561689R00116